DANE

a taboo treat

Mandy,
2 alphas are better
than 1!

♡ K

K WEBSTER

Dane
Copyright © 2018 K Webster
Naughty St. Nick
Copyright © 2017 K Webster

Cover Design: All By Design
Photo: Adobe Stock
Editor: All About the Edits
Formatting: Champagne Book Design

I'm used to being in charge.
In the courtroom. In life. In the bedroom.
But then I met him.

He brings me *literally* to my knees.

Handsome. Charismatic. Sexy as hell.
He's everything I desperately crave to possess.

I'm burning to get him beneath me just to have a taste.
Turns out, though, one taste isn't enough.
And he's starved for me too.

Two alphas fighting for dominance.
He thrives on control and I can't give it up.

A battle of wills.
The bedroom is the battlefield and our hearts are on the line.

DEDICATION

To my husband…
Thank you for being my partner in life, in parent-
hood, and in love.

"If Harry Potter taught us anything it's that no one should live in a closet."

—J.K. Rowling

K WEBSTER'S TABOO WORLD

Welcome to my taboo world! These stories began as an effort to satisfy the taboo cravings in my reader group. The two stories in the duet, *Bad Bad Bad*, were written off the cuff and on the fly for my group. Since everyone seemed to love the stories so much, I expanded the characters and the world. I've been adding new stories ever since. Each book stands alone from the others and doesn't need to be read in any particular order. I hope you enjoy the naughty characters in this town! These are quick reads sure to satisfy your craving for instalove, smokin' hot sex, and happily ever afters!

Bad Bad Bad
Coach Long
Ex-Rated Attraction
Mr. Blakely
Malfeasance
Easton
Crybaby
Lawn Boys
Renner's Rules
The Glue
Dane

Several more titles to be released soon!
Thanks for reading!
K

A Note to the Reader...

Dane started as a short story called *Naughty St. Nick* in the *What Happens During the Holidays* anthology last Christmas. The story was meant to be short and sweet to fit the parameters of the project. However, my dear characters demanded a LOT more of their story, not just the tiny nibble they were originally given. Nearly a year later, I sat down and finally gave them what they wanted. My characters are spoiled and who am I to deny them a thing?

I hope you enjoy reading the rest of their story.

Love Always,
K Webster

DANE

ONE

Dane

Missy DeMarco winks at me from the other end of the bar, and all I can manage is a slight nod of my head. I'm fucking stupid, really. The girl likes to suck dick and has even mentioned she's down for anal. And yet...my head's just not there. You'd think my forty-seven-year-old almost-divorced ass would be into nailing twenty-something blondes with big shiny lips. Instead, I find myself dragging my gaze back to my tumbler filled with amber liquid. I drain my glass and count down the minutes until I can leave this lame-ass party.

Except leaving the firm's Christmas party when you're the managing partner would be highly frowned upon. Not to mention, I'm sure that little

1

tidbit of information would get back to Janice. Shame on me for thinking that after twenty-six years of marriage, she'd show a little kindness my way. Not Janice. She's been a super cunt ever since I said, "I do." When she filed for divorce a few months ago, I knew my life was over. The over-botoxed snob has been trying to bankrupt me ever since.

Thank fuck I'm an attorney. If I were just some run-of-the-mill stupid sap, Janice would have already screwed me so hard I wouldn't be able to sit for years. But I know her bitch ways and I've been able to preempt every one of her attempts to ruin me.

"I'll have whatever he's having," a deep voice booms. "And put it on his tab."

I snort and swivel around to see which asshole is trying to sour my mood even more. When I get a good look at a young guy dressed as Santa, I crack a smile, despite myself. The guy, who can't be any older than twenty, is tall and broad-shouldered. It's the smirk on his face that has me shaking my head in a humorous manner.

"The bad girls are that way, Santa," I say with a grunt, and nod toward where Missy and some of the other paralegals from the office are babbling about God only knows what to my colleagues, who only seem interested in their tits.

Santa chuckles as he sits down on the stool beside me. The bartender hands us our drinks before heading over to someone waving him down. My gaze is pulled back in Santa's direction when he tugs off his cap to run his fingers through his messy light brown hair, that's wild and overgrown. He sets the hat on the bar top and regards me with an impish grin.

"Thanks for the drink, buddy," he says and holds his glass out to me.

The man's brown eyes are sharp and intelligent despite his fucking stupid Christmas outfit. I don't even know him and I know everyone who works at our firm. He must have come with someone as a guest, or perhaps he's someone staying at this hotel who's decided to crash the party.

"Dane," I grunt and clink my glass to his.

"Nick," he replies and leans on his elbow to watch Missy and the gang. I can hear her giggles all the way over here and can't help but cringe.

"Like St. Nick?" I question with a lifted brow. "Clever."

His attention darts back to mine and he shrugs. "Something like that." When he starts working at the buttons on the front of his red suit, I find myself fixated on his strong fingers. He pulls off the jacket and tosses it on the bar. "Fuck, it's hot in here."

I admire his physique. His white T-shirt is molded to his sculpted chest. I've always tried to maintain my body. Hell, it was one of the things Janice would always bitch about. *"You work out too much,"* as if staying fit was a bad thing. I pinch the bridge of my nose and attempt to block out thoughts of her. Even on the verge of finalizing our divorce, she's still controlling my every thought and action.

"We'll have another," Nick hollers to the bartender. "This one's on me. My friend here is having a bad day." He reaches forward and squeezes my shoulder. Awareness prickles through me.

Don't go there, Dane.

Last time I let those feelings get ahold of me, I almost lost my best friend.

"Want to talk about it?" he questions, dragging me from my self-loathing.

I scrub at my scruffy face with one hand and shake my head. "Not really. Why are you over here talking to me anyway?" I turn to see one of Missy's friends making eyes at Nick. "Cassia would love for you to talk to her."

When I look back at him, his lips twitch in

amusement, and I find myself staring at them for longer than necessary. *Goddammit, Dane. Get your head out of your ass.*

"Cassia already tried to talk to me," he says with a groan. "And by talking, I mean, she stuck her hand down the front of my pants and gripped my cock. Told me she'd been a bad little girl."

My cock twitches at the mental image. The bartender drops off a couple more drinks and these, too, get sucked down.

"You didn't want to hit that?" I question, my body starting to feel loose with the alcohol running through my veins.

He laughs, and the sound is rich and deep. "No. God, I have standards, man."

I smile back at him. This guy reminds me of my younger self. Back when I was free. When I was a risk-taker, and did what I wanted without worry of how it affected my life. I was carefree and I loved it.

Fast forward twenty-six years, and I couldn't be more opposite. Everything I do has ripple effects. I don't have the pleasure of doing things for fun and without care of repercussions anymore.

"Wife?"

I cringe at the word. When I see him staring at

the pale circle on my finger, I let out a sigh. I wonder how long it will be until it fades. "Soon-to-be ex."

"Was she a bitch?"

I groan. "You have no idea."

He reaches forward and squeezes my shoulder again. "So, we're celebrating?"

I *don't* tell him that I'm not celebrating at all. I *don't* tell him I'm here because I *have* to be. I *do* tell him, "I guess we are."

His teeth are pearly white as he flashes me another conspiratorial grin. He does this thing my best friend Max Rowe does, where he bites on the inside corner of his bottom lip, as if he's trying to hold back something he desperately wants to say. It endears me to this man because the same mannerism endeared me to my best friend all those years ago.

"Out with it, Nick," I grumble.

He throws his head back and a warm laugh rumbles from him. The sound is nice, and I find myself wishing I were a funnier fuck so I could keep the laughs coming from him. My gaze falls to his Adam's apple and, for a brief moment, I wonder what he tastes like there.

Fuck, the booze is getting to me.

Thoughts of Max from the past coupled with

images of Nick from the present have my cock all sorts of confused. I dart my gaze over to Missy, who's climbing into my newest partner, Chandler Stratton's, lap. I failed to mention Missy is the office skank. Apparently, Chandler is too because I know he has a wife who conveniently doesn't happen to be here tonight.

When I turn around, Nick's features darken. He drains his glass and clanks it to the bar surface. His body leans into mine and the heat from it stirs my cock once again.

"Want to get high?"

I nearly choke on my response. "W-What?"

"The good shit. Upstairs in my room. You coming, or are we going to sit around and watch these losers hang all over each other all night?" He pulls away to smirk at me. "Don't tell me you don't smoke pot."

Back in college, that's all I did. Max was a little more straight-laced than I was, but I was always toking it up between classes. It's a miracle I got my shit together and graduated with good grades.

But I haven't smoked since I married Janice. This is stupid.

"I don't know, man," I mutter.

"How about you think about it?" His lips quirk up on one side. "Room eleven forty-three. When, *not if*, you get tired of these assholes, I'll be upstairs." He snags his Santa stuff and drops a couple of twenties on the bar. "See you in ten."

He saunters away from the bar, and I can't help but stare after him. The T-shirt he's wearing is tight on his body and shows off a muscular back. My traitorous cock twitches again. It's as if it's coming to life after twenty-six years of slumber.

Minutes tick by, and all I can think about is Nick and his easygoing persona. God, what I wouldn't give to get even a quarter of the man I once was back. To be able to fucking crash an office party in a Santa costume and then buddy up to the head guy in charge, only to invite him to smoke pot. Ballsy, this guy. And, at one time, I had balls too. That was before Janice cut them right off my body and stuffed them in her eight-hundred-dollar designer purse. If it hadn't been for Melanie, our daughter, I'd have left her ages ago.

I sneak a glance back at Missy, who's making out with Chandler. This shit will be all over the office on Monday. Better him than me, though. The last thing I need is for Janice getting ahold of that little piece of ammo. Chandler's wife is *his* problem.

Without thinking too long on it, I make a decision. Tonight, I'll be Dane from college. I'll stop worrying the fuck over everything in my life and go get
my ass high with Santa Claus. I slap some cash down
on the bar and slip away from my employees, who are
all behaving rather badly. I don't need to see Ronald
from payroll sucking face with my secretary, Elaine.
And I don't even want to know what her fiancé will
think when somebody inevitably records that shit on
video and sends it to him.

Christmas office parties suck.

I stride out of the bar and head toward the bank
of elevators. The night is fairly young. I could go to
my room on the fifteenth floor, buy some overpriced
porn, and jack off so I can go to sleep. Or…

The elevators open, and I step in. My finger hov-
ers over the number fifteen before dropping to punch
in the eleven. The split-second decision has several bricks of stress falling off my back. A night alone
with my fist isn't going to ease the tension like getting
stoned with Santa will.

I'm smirking all the way to his door. When I
raise my hand to knock, I hesitate and drop it. This
is probably stupid. I don't even know this guy. What

if he—

The door swings open and Nick laughs. "Dude, don't stand outside the door like a fuckin' stalker. Come in."

I snort and shake my head. "Where's the suit?" I'm trying to keep my features impassive, but he's traded his Santa shit for a pair of gray sweatpants that hang low on his hips. Nick is no longer wearing a shirt, and his tanned chest muscles are on full display. His messy hair hangs in front of his sharp eyes as a knowing smile teases his lips. *Goddamn, I need to stop looking at those lips.*

"I was getting hot," he says as he saunters over to the bed and stretches out. His stomach muscles are tight and defined. He probably spends about as much time in the gym as I do, but I sure as hell don't have his oblique muscles. Lucky young bastard. I want to ask him about his workout regime but then decide that probably sounds gay.

And I'm definitely not gay.

He clears his throat, and I realize I've been staring at his stomach for the past minute like a fucking creeper. This should be my cue to leave, to save myself any further embarrassment.

"Man, lighten up," he says with a grin. "Take

your jacket off and stay awhile. But no ties allowed. Ties are for uptight assholes, and we're about to get stoned as fuck."

I chuckle and am thankful he blows off my odd behavior. With my back to him, I shrug out of my jacket and hang it on the back of the desk chair. Then, as requested, I remove the tie and toss it over as well. After unbuttoning the top couple of buttons, I roll up the sleeves on my dress shirt. When I turn back to him, he's watching me with a guarded expression.

"The fridge is filled with every poison you can think of," he tells me as he grabs a tray from his end table. He starts stuffing weed into a small metal pipe. "I'll take some Cuervo."

I give him a slight nod before fetching some mini bottles from the fridge. I set them down on his table just as he takes a hit. He grabs my wrist below my expensive watch and squeezes. Then, he reaches up and hands me the pipe.

"Tell me that's not the best shit ever," he says with a grin as he looks up at me. With his hand on my wrist and a smile that probably gets him whatever the fuck he wants, I can't help but admit my attraction to him. My body is practically buzzing with barely controlled desire. I thought I worked through this shit decades ago. All it takes is one good-looking guy to touch me and smile, and I'm ready to explore again.

Except, the last time I did a little exploring, my best friend gave me a punch to the face, and I almost ended our friendship.

"Smoke the weed, Dane," he growls, jerking me from my inner hatred. "Your mind works all the time, huh? Never shuts off? You've got to take some moments to just breathe, man. Wear the fucking Santa suit. Smoke the weed. Go after the guy with the five o'clock shadow and perpetual scowl who's better off without his bitch wife."

I take the pipe and frown at him.

He shrugs and pulls his hand away. "I'm enjoying a little last hurrah myself actually, before I join the frowning bastards club."

Something about his words irritates me. I had that same attitude so long ago. Like the fun was over once college ended and it was time to do right by my parents. Career. Wife. Kids. And I did. I followed the fucking rules. For what?

I inhale the smoke and let it fill my lungs. It's been ages since the last time I got high, but God, how I missed it. I close my eyes and let the weed do its job. When I reopen them, Nick is smirking at me.

"You should sit your big ass down, old man, before you pass the fuck out."

I laugh and hand him the pipe. "Fine, but I'm sitting there." I tip my head to the place on the bed beside him. "I'm not trying to put the fucking moves on you. I just want to sit someplace besides the uncomfortable looking desk chair."

His brown eyes narrow and the corner of his mouth twitches in amusement. "Whatever you say."

I kick off my shoes and saunter around to the other side of the bed. Once I'm stretched out next to him, he hands me the pipe again. The weed is good and it's already loosening me up. I feel myself smiling more than I have in a long ass time.

"Got any kids?" he asks as I inhale.

With a long exhale and a huge plume of smoke surrounding me, I nod. "Mel. She's fucking adorable. I love that kid."

"How old?"

"About your age." I cringe the moment the words leave my mouth.

He seems nonplussed. "Twenty-five?"

"Almost twenty-six, actually."

Jesus Christ. I'm attracted to some kid who is younger than my daughter. I want to silently berate myself, but then he hands me one of the bottles of liquor.

"Drink up, old man."

I growl. "Stop calling me that."

He laughs and fuck if I don't laugh too.

TWO

Dane

I down my third mini liquor bottle in a row and wave off the weed when Nick tries to hand it to me again. I'm higher than a fucking kite right now. And he's right, this room is hot.

"Fuck," I complain. "It's like a sauna in here."

He smirks and sits up. "Maybe you should take off all that armor."

My nostrils flare when he reaches forward and takes it upon himself to start unbuttoning my shirt. I can't breathe or move for fear of letting my attraction to him show.

"I'm gay," he rumbles in a low voice that makes my cock thicken in my boxers.

I blurt out my words. "I'm not." As soon as they come out, I feel stupid. Like a fucking bigot asshole redneck. Here I am, claiming I'm not gay, but I've been thinking about this guy's lips since the moment he spoke. And every time he speaks or touches me, my cock responds. If that isn't gay, I don't know what is.

"I 'wasn't' once either," he tells me, as he slowly continues unbuttoning my shirt. When he reaches the bottom, he tugs my shirt from my pants. A groan escapes me, and I have to close my eyes to hide the need burning in my eyes.

"Nick," I warn.

He leans back on the bed. "I was just unbuttoning your shirt, man, not accidentally poking my dick against your ass."

I pop my eyes open and turn to glare at him. My cock is straining in my slacks, but I will it to settle. I'm met with a challenging stare from him.

"Have you ever had your dick sucked by a guy?" he questions. His jaw clenches as his gaze skirts down my body to where my dick is trying to join the party.

"No," I grit out and sit up. I yank the shirt off because now I'm sweating. The wife-beater I was wearing under my dress shirt gets torn off and tossed away too. When I lean back against the pillows, his gaze is on my chest.

"You lift a lot?"

Pride surges through me. Janice couldn't ever take time out of her precious day to notice my physique. You don't have a body like mine at almost fifty without working your ass off daily for it.

"I do," I grunt.

"It shows, old man." He grins at me, and I'll be damned if I don't nearly come in my pants. *God, this is so fucked up.*

"You in college?" I question, in an attempt to change the subject.

His smile falls and he shakes his head. Nick is sexy when he's all grins and mystery. The look he's giving me now is as though I just stole his puppy. And, fuck me, do I want to give him the damn puppy back.

"Not anymore."

"What's next?"

He sighs. "Corporate world. Fun times."

I scratch at my scruff and frown. "What would you rather be doing? It's written all over your face. You'd rather be doing something else."

Guilt flashes in his eyes. "It doesn't matter. It's done."

I reach over and brush my knuckles against his firm chest. "It matters."

17

His breath hitches and he affixes me with a heated stare that does nothing to calm my cock. I'm normally bold with women, not men. After Janice and I separated, I took my fair share of women to bed. I was always the initiator. This feels different. Unchartered territory.

"I love computers. In college, I took a ton of courses when I could. They didn't relate to my degree, but I didn't care. I love taking them apart and putting them back together again. I fix them when they break and break them when they're fixed, only to turn around and make them better. My brain tends to be more mechanical than anything else." He sighs and shrugs. "But it's just for fun."

I don't stop running my knuckles along the grooves of his abs. "The world needs computer engineers and they make good money. I don't understand why you don't do that."

He rolls off the bed and stalks over to the fridge. When he bends over, I admire his sculpted ass in his sweatpants. I don't know what the fuck I'm doing, but lying on this bed talking to—touching—this man makes me feel better than I've felt in a long time. I don't want to piss the guy off.

I get up and stride over to him. "I didn't mean to

pry." My voice is husky, and he stiffens when I place my palm on his lower back. "The last thing I wanted to do was piss you off."

He stands and turns to look at me. We're evenly matched on height. My shoulders are slightly wider but his are more muscular. The guy has age on his side for sure.

"Have you ever had your cock sucked by a man?" he asks again, his voice sharp.

I glower at him. "No."

"The answer is *not yet*." He licks his bottom lip and then gives me one of those half-ass crooked smiles that make my cock ache.

"I'm not gay," I bite out.

He steps forward and kicks the fridge door shut. When his big hand rubs against my cock through my slacks, I let out a long groan of pleasure. My eyes fall shut as I give in to the delicious sensations of him rubbing on me.

"The answer," he breathes against my lips, "is *not yet*."

Soft lips brush against mine. His lips are real— not like the botoxed shit Janice had. And his kiss is needy in nature, as if he's been waiting to do this all night. One of his hands slides around the back of my neck to hold me in place as he deepens the kiss. His tongue is hot and powerful as it thrusts into my mouth. I haven't been kissed like this in forever.

"Nick," I grunt against his mouth. "I'm not...this is..." But his hand squeezes around my cock through my clothes, and I thrust against him. "Fuck."

"Fuck is right," he growls, and nips at my bottom lip with his teeth. "Undo your belt, old man. I want to suck your cock."

I open my eyes so I can glare at him. He's doing that sexy little thing where he bites on the inside corner of his bottom lip, and it makes me crazy horny. Long ago, I remember feeling like Max was into me the same way I was into him. I'd leaned in and kissed his handsome mouth after one too many shots of vodka one night. It took everything in me to get up the nerve. And that fucker pushed me away. Then, he clocked me right in the jaw. Thankfully, we moved past it, and he's still my closest friend to this day, but that moment hurt my pride more than my jaw. It's one that will stay with me forever. I fell into the arms of the next chick I ran across. I knocked Janice up and the rest was history.

This time, when I lean in to kiss that mouth, I'm met with mirrored desire. I grip Nick's face on both sides and hold him in place while I kiss him hard. Deft fingers are soon on my belt. I never answered him, and he's taking my silence as permission.

I'm not gay.

I'm not gay.

I had a wife, and we made a fucking baby, for crying out loud.

Not.

Gay.

My pants drop to my ankles, and his hand dives into my boxers. Whatever thoughts I was having have long since dissipated. All I can focus on is the powerful way he grips my dick, like no other person besides myself has ever had the strength to do. His hand is rough—not soft like the women I've been with. It feels so fucking good.

"Nick…"

He pulls away and flashes me that impish grin of his that makes me crazy with need. "I'm going to suck your cock now, old man. You're going to stop worrying your ass off over stupid shit and you're going to fucking enjoy it. Got it?"

I grit my teeth and give him a clipped nod.

He drops to a knee and wastes no time pulling my boxers down my thighs. His breath is hot near my dick, and it twitches. I watch with interest as this man takes me in his grip. It was something I fantasized over for a long time. I remember having wet dreams about my friends from junior high and high school sucking my dick. I'd thought every teenager shared the same feelings.

His tongue slides in a circular motion on the tip of my cock, which makes me hiss in pleasure, and I can't help but grasp his hair. I've gripped plenty of long-haired women but never a man. Everything about this is new but so fucking hot. He pumps my cock, much like I would, but faster and stronger. It has me seeing stars. But when his mouth slides down my shaft, I let out a groan and I thrust against him. He must sense what I want because he releases my cock and grips my thighs. I buck slowly into his mouth and revel in the way his teeth scrape against my thick cock. His mouth is larger than any woman I've been with and he takes me easily.

"Fuck," I hiss out. My legs are shaking with the need to skull fuck this stranger. He lets out an animalistic growl that rumbles its way up my cock to my heavy balls, and I give in to my desires. I push the tip of my cock down the back of his tight, hot throat, and the sexy asshole takes it without gagging. Janice refused to suck cock—so selfish—and the other chicks lately seem to half-ass it.

Nick takes cock like a champ.

He bobs along my shaft, his throat open and accepting, and digs his strong fingers into my thighs so hard I'm sure he'll bruise me. The pleasure is too much. It's not just the sensations but the act itself. I'm face fucking a guy who was dressed as Santa not two hours ago. Someone who is practically a kid younger than my daughter. I'm not even divorced yet and I've already hopped the fence and started fucking with guys.

Not guys.

Just this one.

An image of my cock pressing into the hole of his ass has my climax nearing. I'm not gay, I guess, but maybe I fucking am. The very idea of plowing into this man's ass has me blowing my load suddenly and without warning.

Instead of gagging like a fucking girl, he groans, as if my cum is goddamned delicious. Sucks it down like it's the best damn thing he's ever tasted. My legs quiver from exertion and, for a brief moment, I don't worry about anything. In an affectionate move, I run my fingers through his hair.

"That was fucking amazing."

He slides off my cock and affixes me with a naughty smile. "We're just getting started, old man. I haven't even been in your ass yet."

I stare at him, stunned. "*My* ass?"

He stands up and boldly pushes his sweatpants down. My gaze falls to his impressive cock. Long. Hard. Veiny as fuck. I lick my lips because I suddenly have the urge to taste him too. I've never sucked cock before but, fuck, I'm willing to give it a go.

"Hey," he says with a chuckle. "Hungry Eyes. My face is here."

I snap my attention to his. "I've never sucked a man's dick."

"I'll teach you." He winks at me. "But you're not sucking my cock. Not right now. Right now, you're going to bend over that bed and open that ass so I can stick my cock inside."

Heat rushes down across my flesh straight to my dick, which rises instantly. When I was with Janice, it took forever to get hard again after the first time. And now, I'm as virile as the kid in front of me. My dick is ready to play some more.

"Janice says anal hurts," I murmur, my gaze falling back down to where he strokes himself.

"Sounds like Janice was a pussy," he growls. "Are you a pussy, old man?"

I step out of my clothes at my ankles and shove him away. "Does it look like I'm a pussy?"

His gaze travels down my solid chest to where my still-wet cock bobs with excitement. "Your cock misses me already," he taunts.

"Maybe my cock wants in *your* ass," I challenge. I don't let my self-doubt creep in. This is all new territory, and I hope I'm doing it right. If he were a woman, I'd have no problems talking dirty and I sure as hell wouldn't doubt myself. It takes everything in me to silence my inner voice, who thinks I'm not good enough or young enough or fucking *gay* enough for this man.

He smirks and saunters over to his suitcase on the floor. When he bends over, I get a nice view of his perfect ass and heavy balls hanging between his thighs. I groan and grip my aching cock. I *do* want to put my cock in his ass. I've never been so sure about wanting something. I stalk over to him and grab his hips. He straightens to his full height but doesn't move away. My cock rubs against his crack. Fuck, it feels good.

"Down boy," he jokes. "You got yours. Now it's time to get mine. If you still want more after that, I'll give you what you want." He turns in my arms and flashes me a smoldering grin as he pokes my chest with a bottle of lube. That smile will get him whatever the fuck he wants, goddammit.

"Talk me through this," I grunt.

He reaches up and grips the side of my neck. Our mouths fuse together again and all apprehension disappears. When this man kisses me, he makes me lose myself in him. He's got skills, I'll give him that.

We kiss until I'm dying for another release. He pulls away, and his voice is husky and demanding as he growls, "Get on the bed, old man."

THREE

Dane

I run my fingers through my hair and attempt to shake away my nerves. I'm doing this. I'm really fucking doing this. A lifetime of fantasies is coming true in one night. I'm hesitant to go down this path completely because I'm worried there will be no coming back. I may not fess up to being gay, but this certainly makes me at least bisexual. The idea of stuffing my cock back inside Missy's slippery cunt doesn't have the same appeal anymore. I've tasted the forbidden fruit and I want the whole damn tree now.

"Dane," he grumbles and gives me a shove onto the bed. "Get on your knees and give me your virgin ass."

His words light a fire inside me, and my cock jolts. "Fuck, you're bossy."

He smirks and winks. "I like being in charge."

"So do I," I grumble, but climb onto the bed, eyeing him over my shoulder. The man is a fucking god, all chiseled and shit. Those oblique muscles…Jesus, I want them on my body in more ways than one.

His lips quirk up on one side. "Anyone ever tell you that you have a nice ass?"

"Missy," I reply with a laugh.

"Missy is a whore."

I shrug because I can't disagree there. "My ass isn't nearly as hairy as yours."

"Bend over, smart mouth," he growls.

My nerves are tight with anticipation but I obey this young thing who has me about to explode with my orgasm all over this hotel bed. The bed dips as he climbs on behind me. His palm is warm on my ass.

"Relax, old man. This is going to feel good."

I exhale and nod as he pops open the cap on the lube. The squirting sound unnerves me. I'm rethinking my decision when he rubs the tip of his finger down my ass crack. A shiver rumbles through me.

"Stroke your cock," he orders.

I groan and grip my throbbing thickness with one hand. Gently, he pushes his finger inside my hole. It doesn't hurt—just feels different. When he starts moving it in and out, I let out a hiss of air.

Okay…

Fuck.

This does feel good.

"You like that, old man?"

"Hell yeah," I grunt and push my ass against his finger, meeting him thrust for thrust. "It's not enough, though."

"You're a virgin, big boy," he says with a laugh. "I have to get this tight ass ready for me. You've seen the size of my dick. Let's get you stretched out first before you start begging for my cock."

I chuckle, but then he starts working another finger inside my ass. It burns a little, but I like it. I'd assumed I would feel less manly or some shit, but with my dick in my hand and jolts of pleasure zapping through me from deep within, I don't give a fuck about societal ideologies. All I care about is feeling good.

He works me in some goddamned magical way that has me loosening my grip on my cock so I don't spurt my orgasm all over the bed. I want to save it for my turn. I *will* get my turn.

"Your ass was made for this," he tells me, his free hand affectionately gripping my hip. "I'm going to try another finger."

I tense in anticipation, which only makes me completely aware of the foreign fingers inside me. With a deep breath, I relax again just as he starts pushing another digit inside me.

Fuck, my ass is full, and it gives me an idea of what his cock will feel like. A thrilling shudder courses through me. He stills and caresses my lower back.

"You're doing great, man," he praises, his voice low and husky. "I'm so turned on right now."

I risk a glance over my shoulder, and sure enough, raw lust is shining in his eyes. It turns me on too. "I want your cock," I growl.

He smirks, which makes me clench my ass. Pleasure surges through me. "Let me suit up, old man. Sit tight." His fingers slide out of me, and goddammit, I feel so empty. I stare at the hotel sheets and wait for him to come back. I'm afraid to move in the event this all really is some fucked-up fantasy. If I wake up and I'm in bed with Janice, I'll fucking die.

"This first time," he tells me as he climbs back on the bed, "you may not come. It might hurt. If you don't come, we'll swap places and you can get off. It's all about give and take. I don't believe in that top and bottom shit. I like receiving just as much as I like giving. And, old man, I want you to like both too." His palm slaps my ass, and I grunt. When I glare at him over my shoulder, he laughs. "Calm down, killer. You'll get your turn to pay me back."

He rips open the foil, and I once again hear the sound of the lube getting squirted out. Then, his fingers knead my ass cheeks as his slippery cock slides against my balls. It's the most unusual sensation, but I love it. I fucking love it.

"That feels…"

I can hear the grin in his voice. "I know."

He removes one of his hands from my ass and then his tip starts rubbing against my hole. I grunt because I don't like the teasing and push against him. He's thick but I want him. All of him.

"So eager," he growls. "Once you've had my dick in your ass, you'll never want sex with a woman again."

Somehow, I believe his words wholeheartedly. It should scare the fuck out of me, but at this point in my life, I don't think I care anymore. I want to do what makes me happy. Having Nick in my ass makes me happy.

He pushes slowly into me and a delicious fire burns through me as he enters me inch by slow inch.

It's too much but it's not enough. I want it. I want it all. He slides the rest of the way in and his balls slap against mine. The sensation is intense and sends ripples of pleasure zapping through me. Fucking Janice or Missy or any of those other one-night stands in the past few months never felt this good. Sure, I came every time, but I never felt pleasure like this.

"God," I hiss. "This is—"

He slams into me, effectively cutting off my words, and I roar as I fist the sheets. Pain mixed with pleasure pulsates through me. It fucking intoxicates me. Each time he thrusts forward, his heavy balls hit mine, and I nearly blow my load. With that thought, I release my cock and grip the sheets with both fists. I don't want to come yet.

"Your ass is so tight," he praises. "So fucking tight."

Grunts and slaps echo in the hotel room. This virile young man fucks me hard and without apology. I wouldn't want it any other way. Pleasure builds up within me—deep inside me—and I crave to grip my cock so I can come. I know it will be intense.

But…

I want in his ass too.

"Fuck," he grunts as he loses control. "Fuck!"

His cock seems to double in size as he throbs out

his release. It's intense and feels fucking amazing. I clench my ass which makes him hiss, and a grin pulls at my lips. I may be under him but I like that I can control his cock with one simple movement. He pulls out suddenly, and I growl.

"Your hole is as wide as my cock right now," he marvels. "Fucking beautiful."

His fingers push back inside me as if to prove his point. When he fondles my balls at the same time, I nearly come right then.

"Nick," I snarl. "Get your fine ass on this bed so I can fuck it. I'm tired of waiting."

His laughter is loud and boyish, causing me to smile. "Who's the boss now?"

He pulls his fingers out of me and strides off to the bathroom. I roll onto my back and stare up at the ceiling as he washes up. When I stepped into my firm's Christmas party tonight, I did not expect to end the night with some random guy drilling my ass. I start laughing as Nick comes sauntering back into the room. He's disposed of the condom and has another one in his hand.

"What's so funny?" he questions with a sexy quirk of his brow.

"I just didn't expect the night to end like this," I

admit with a sigh. "Come here."

He climbs over me and straddles my thighs. My cock bounces back to life when he tears open the foil with his teeth. Nick expertly rolls the rubber down over my cock before he spits on the tip and wets the condom. Then, he crawls over until he's at my hips. His brown eyes are hard with fire and lust and desire. I like when this playful guy grows serious for me. It sure as hell beats the annoyed stares Janice used to give.

"Guide your dick inside me," he instructs.

"Bossy," I chide with a grin as I grip my cock. "Even from on top."

"I have to get this bossiness out of my system. Come Monday, I answer to the man." He smirks until my much thicker cock presses against his tight hole. We both groan when he eases himself down over me.

I've been in countless women—even a few of their asses—in my time. But, Jesus fucking Christ, it has never felt this good. I hiss once he's completely seated on me. Reaching forward, I grab his cock that's hardening pretty quickly despite just coming. I start jerking at him in conjunction with the way he bounces on my dick.

"You're so big," he groans.

"Biggest cock that's been in your ass?"

He does that sexy-as-fuck lip biting thing, and I growl.

"Yeah. Fuck yeah," he admits. "I should have used lube, old man."

This time, I'm the one throwing a smug grin his way. "I'm going to tear up that ass."

Lust swims in his eyes. I grip the side of his neck and roll us over until I'm on top. We adjust, and then I'm driving into him without mercy. His full lips part as he groans in pleasure. I wrap my hand around his fist as he strokes his dick. Our eyes meet, and I'm grounded in this moment. It's as if my life makes perfect sense. I've been searching a lifetime for such a physical and mental connection with someone.

It's just with a man, not a woman like I'd once thought.

"Dane," he breathes. "Yes. God, yes."

I thrust hard until I'm cursing him for being so fucking perfect. "Goddamn you for ruining my life," I snarl. I come deep inside of him as he lets out a hiss of his own. His climax shoots all over his chest. Once we're both finished rattling with our release, I press my forehead against his. "Goddamn you for changing everything."

His fingers stroke through my hair. "You're not exactly the fuck-and-run type of guy, are you?"

I growl and nip at his lip. Now that I've had him, I don't want to lose this. I want more. There's so much more I want to explore with him.

"You're not going anywhere," I murmur against his mouth.

He kisses me back softly. "Then you're ruining my life too."

I narrow my eyes at him. "How's that?"

"I don't exactly do relationships."

I smirk. "And I don't exactly do men."

"Yet here we are," we both say and then laugh.

"Come on, St. Nick," I tell him as I slide out of his tight body. "Let's get cleaned up and order some food. I'm starving. And then"—I point at his limp dick—"you're going to get that hard again and show me how to suck it."

FOUR

Dane

We never made it to him showing me how to suck his dick. Hell, we barely made it through a shower before he had me bent over the bathroom counter and was fucking me again. My cock was spent and refused to get back up, but he pushed deep inside, forcing pleasure from places I didn't even know could feel good. I'd come all over the sink and my dick wasn't even hard. Riddle me that one.

"Tell me about your family," I murmur, my fingers trailing along his sculpted arm in the darkness of the room. We've long since turned off the lights and crawled into bed but neither of us can sleep.

"My dad is a demanding prick. Mom is a selfish cunt. My little sister Christina is the golden child," he says, a hint of bitterness in his tone.

"And what are you?"

"The family fuck-up. The gay son who was supposed to give my parents a daughter-in-law and grandkids. Instead, I give them ulcers."

I hug him to me and kiss his forehead. "You just graduated from college, though, right? You're doing something admirable."

He shrugs. I'm becoming fond of his shrugs. "A semester early too. They don't see that, though. It's never enough for my dad. Always pushing for perfection."

I know exactly how he feels. "You don't *have* to do what he wants."

He tugs away from me and reaches for something on the end table. His lighter illuminates his face as he lights his pipe and takes a hit. He doesn't offer it to me but rather puts it to my lips. I inhale it and let it flow through me, calming me to a sleepy state.

"I don't know that I am ready to buck against my dad," he admits.

He takes another hit and we sit in silence for a moment.

"I think you should try," I tell him and lie on my side to face him. My fingers run along his cut stomach. "Fuck your dad."

He chuckles. "Yeah, fuck my dad."

I rest my palm on his lower stomach and run my thumb along his happy trail. "When I'm sober, I might not be this cool."

His fingers stroke my hair as he takes another hit. "But you'll still like cock."

I snort but let my eyes drift closed. "You're probably right about that."

I wake because my phone is blaring from the end table. The sun is bright and my head is throbbing something terrible. When I start to reach for the obnoxious sound, I can't move. Someone heavy is sprawled out over me, like a koala hugging a tree. The night before comes flooding through me the moment I see a hard, tanned shoulder lying across me. Manly snores rumble from my big-ass koala, and I think he's drooling on me. I grin because he's cute when he's not being all domineering as hell.

My phone is going off again, which pisses me off because I wanted to enjoy a few more moments like this. Instead, I'm sliding out from under him to answer it.

"What?" I grit out.

I scratch my balls as I climb out of bed and head to the bathroom to take a piss.

"You don't have to be rude, Dane," Janice snips out.

My morning boner is gone from hearing her voice. I can't believe I fucked her for most of my adult life. "What do you want?" I grumble as I take a leak.

"Are you peeing while on the phone? Ugh," she groans. "I do not miss that at all. Anyway, Melanie wants us all over at her house for Christmas. She's asked we play nicely. I'm bringing a date." Her voice is low and deadly, as if she assumes this will piss me off.

"Lovely. Anything else?"

She huffs. "So, you have to come for our daughter and you can't be rude to my date."

"Honestly, Janice," I bite out. "I don't give a fuck about you or your date. As long as I don't have to talk to you, I'm happy. Tell Mel I love her and I'll see her then."

I hang up the phone and finish up in the bathroom. Once my hands are clean, I snag one of the condoms from the end table and roll it on my cock. Just the sight of Nick's curved naked ass on the bed has me hard again. I squirt some lube on my cock and make sure it's smeared all over before I climb in behind him. He continues to snore, even as I tease my cock along the crack of his ass. But when I start sucking on his neck and shoulder, his breathing becomes quiet.

"Sneak attack?" His voice is deep and gravelly. It's hot as hell.

"Had to catch your bossy ass off guard," I tell him with a grin before nipping at his flesh.

I grip my throbbing dick and push against his tight hole. His body seems to suck my dick into him slowly. A hiss leaves my lips as I push fully into him. Last night was amazing. This morning, without the haze of the alcohol or drugs, is fucking epic.

"You're insatiable," he groans. "Couldn't this wait until lunch, old man?"

"I'm hungry now."

He lets out a moan when I thrust harder into him. I wrap my arm around him and latch my fingers with his. My thrusts are jagged and uneven but each one sends pleasure coursing through me. I nip at his ear and throat as he guides our hands to his cock. Together, we stroke his big dick while I fuck him from behind. It doesn't take long until we're both grunting. He comes first with a loud groan, and I follow behind with a hiss.

"You're not a morning person, are you?" I tease with a chuckle.

He grumbles. "Nope."

"How's that going to work for you in the corporate world?"

"It's not. My boss is going to hate me."

I run my tongue along the flesh near his ear. "When your boss sees your tight ass in a pair of khakis, I can guarantee he won't fucking care if you stroll in late."

He laughs but then swats at me. "Go away and let me sleep."

I start rubbing at his soft cock until it starts hardening again. I'm still deep in his ass and I need to switch out condoms, but I like working up my sleeping bear.

"This isn't how 'gay' works," he grumbles.

I laugh. "How does it work?"

"You're not supposed to fuck me eighty times in one night."

"You woke the beast. It's all your fault," I tease.

"Tell him to go to sleep."

"Text me. Don't be a stranger."

We traded numbers but didn't make promises. We fucked and talked about nothing serious and got high. The entire weekend. And now…

"Peterson file is on your desk," Elaine chirps when I walk in on Monday. Despite her chirping, her eyes are bloodshot from crying and she isn't wearing her engagement ring. Firm Christmas parties always leave a path of destruction.

Normally, I spend the following few days listening to Janice half-heartedly apologize for flirting with half my staff. This year, the destruction is in my mind. I can't stop thinking about *him*.

Chandler pops into my office behind me just as I stroll inside. He's been here a few months as our newest partner but I haven't gotten to know him well. His partnership is contracted on a trial basis to make sure we're a good fit first.

"Morning," he says in a false cheerful tone. It gets under my skin. I haven't had enough coffee to deal with fake shit today.

"Yep. What's up?" I demand, cutting straight to the point. "I have court in two hours, which means I have work to do."

He scrubs his fingers across his face and gives me

a guilty stare. "Sorry about Missy."

I shoot him an annoyed glance as I start thumbing through my file. "What about Missy?"

"I know you and her were, um…" he says with a huff. "Together."

At this, I laugh, and it comes out harsh. "Hardly. I don't recall fucking her a few weekends in a row, *together.*" I pin him with a glare. "Is that all?" I don't even razz him about being married and sleeping with my most recent fuck buddy.

He sits his bulky ass in the seat in front of my desk despite my just telling him I have shit to do. A stormy look crosses over his features. "I can't get ahold of him. I'm sorry."

I stare at him in confusion. "What?"

"My son."

"The new hire?"

I dart my gaze over to the clock. Ten after eight. "Are you worried he's hurt?"

This time, he's the one frowning. "No. But I'm going to hurt him for being late."

"It's only ten after," I tell him. "Lighten up."

"It's his first day," he growls.

I pinch the bridge of my nose. "I don't have time for this."

"I know, and that's why I'm apologizing," he huffs.

"No. I don't have time for"—I wave my hand between us—"*this*."

He apologizes again before he leaves.

A mountain of work lies before me, but I ignore it all to text Nick.

Me: How's corporate world?

His response is immediate.

Nick: Fucking bland. You should see this place.

Me: I can only imagine. Where is this new place at? If it's downtown, we should grab some burgers for lunch.

"Mr. Alexander," Elaine interrupts from my doorway. "Mr. Stratton's son is here. Should I send him straight to HR or did you want to meet him first?"

Nick: I actually just passed a burger place walking in. Send me the address. I'll find out what time I can leave.

I'm just about to respond when Elaine ushers in a man. The guy is tall and muscular. His jaw is chiseled and his longish hair has been combed back and styled neatly. Black-rimmed glasses sit perched on his nose. He wears a sharp gray suit and he has one hand in his pocket, which makes the material hug his sculpted ass. A half grin plays at his lips as he looks at his phone.

I am fucked.

"Nicholas Stratton?"

We're just Dane and Nick. Not Dane Alexander, managing partner, and Nicholas Stratton, our newest attorney. *Fuck*.

Upon hearing my voice, his eyes jerk over to mine and genuine surprise morphs over his features. I stand and fully take him in. If I thought he was hot naked and in bed, that was before the man was donning an expensive suit and wearing a cocky lawyer attitude.

"Mr. Alexander."

"Elaine," I grunt. "Excuse us. I'll take it from here. Close the door behind you."

As soon as she's gone, I storm over to him. The first thing I do is grab his jaw in my brutal grip. I can't help but notice how hot he looks in his glasses.

"You used me?" I seethe.

His brows scrunch together in confusion. "What? Fuck no."

"But the Christmas party? You finding me and…" I trail off and dart my gaze to the door, as if someone will hear all about my weekend homosexual rendezvous. "All an act to get closer to the boss?"

He swats my hand away and glares. Fuck, if it

doesn't turn me on. "No, old man, I did not use you. My dad wanted me to come mingle with people I'd be working with. I figured the boss man—*Mr. Alexander, as I knew him*—was over with him as he flirted with anyone who wasn't my mother. You were just some lonely hot guy in a bar who I wanted to know. How the hell was I supposed to know you were the managing partner?"

My gaze drops to his lips and I lick mine. God, he smells exceptionally good this morning. I don't know what sort of cologne he has on, but I'm going to get myself some because I like it that much.

"This is fucked up," I growl, my hands running up the front of his solid chest inside his suit jacket. "I'm your boss."

He grabs my hard cock through my slacks. "And in the bedroom, *I'm* still the boss."

FIVE

Nick

F uck.

Only I could manage to screw up something this bad. My dad is going to shit himself when he finds out I'm sleeping with Dane Alexander. Managing partner, and essentially my dad's boss. *My* boss.

I remove my hand from Dane's impressive cock and take a step back. So often, I'm impulsive and go with what feels right. Hardly ever do I consider the ripple effects of my actions.

Until now.

If I mess up this job, I'll be messing up my father's too. My sister Christina and my mother will be impacted if this all blows up. Pulling off my glasses, I scrub my palm down my face before placing them back on my nose. Dane's jaw is clenched, the muscles there ticking, as his cock strains against his slacks. His hands are fisted and he stares intently at me.

"I'm sorry," I groan. "That was out of line."

Dane's graphite-colored eyes narrow. Over the weekend, I'd marveled at how gray his penetrating stare was. Like a thunderstorm racing across the sky, chasing off any hints of dark blue. When he smiles, though, the storm clears and they seem more blue than gray.

He's not smiling now.

In fact, he's still pissed.

"I didn't mean for any of this to happen," I mutter. "I'm just here to do my job. I told you I'm more of a 'keep it casual' kind of guy." The words are true but they don't feel right on my tongue. I've sought out solace in another's hot flesh beneath the sheets more often than I'd like to admit. This past weekend was the first time I considered that maybe what I'd been searching for was right in front of me.

I knew that shit was too good to be true.

"I have some cases to work on before court today, but I think we should still take that lunch. Talk a little more about this," he says, finally. His gaze has softened and he doesn't look like he wants to kill me. Progress.

"Sure," I say, shrugging one shoulder. "I'll see you around."

He gives me a nod. "Go see HR, and then make sure your dad settles you in at your office. Your assistant is named Susan. She takes care of Dorian Rowe too."

I turn away and start toward the door when he calls out, stopping me once more.

"I like the glasses, Nick."

A smile tugs at my lips. "Bye, Dane."

As soon as the door closes behind me, I walk over to HR after some nice people help me along the way. After an hour of filling out paperwork and the woman droning on about the firm's policies, my dad knocks on the door, interrupting us. For once, I'm happy to see him. My dad—Chandler Stratton—was always someone I wanted to be. That is, until I turned thirteen, and I'd walked in on him kissing our neighbor. They played it off but then later that night, he and my mom fought. Things were thrown. Mom sobbed hysterically. Dad apologized. But at that moment, a bitter seed was planted in my belly. It's grown wildly ever since.

My dad is a cheating dick who holds everyone up to impossible standards, unapologetically so. Mom,

I've learned, is weak. She turns a blind eye to every one of his affairs, and last year, I learned she was having one of her own. The only reason they stay married, I'm convinced, is because they don't want the embarrassment of being separated, especially for Christina. She's a senior in high school and heavily involved in everything. My parents, albeit selfish people, have unselfishly stayed together for her benefit.

"This being late stuff has to stop, Nick," Dad says, once we're out of earshot of HR.

"I was late once," I grumble.

"Your first day. It made me look bad in front of Dane," he complains.

I don't mention Dane was the reason I was late. That sure as fuck isn't happening. I'm not giving Dad any ammunition as far as that goes. We've gone round and round about my sexual orientation. I'm too fucking tired to do that shit today, and then load on top of that how I screwed his boss…not happening.

"Sorry."

He shoots me a disappointed look before letting his face morph into the handsome grin that lures in every female in the vicinity. "Dorian," he says into the office. "Meet my son, Nicholas Stratton."

I step through the door and my eyes land on a

pretty blonde woman. All behind her desk on the credenza are family pictures. She appears to be married to a man around the same age as Dane. A pang of jealousy slices through me. It seems everyone has a happy family. Except me. Dad continually makes sure of that.

"Nice to meet you, Nicholas," she says as she stands, making her way over to me.

I shake her hand. "Nick. Call me Nick."

"Chandler's son, huh?" Her brow lifts and I see the look in her eyes. Trying to gauge whether or not I'm just like him, I'm sure.

"Yep," I grit out, forcing a smile.

The wrinkles in her brow smooth out. "I'm sorry," she teases.

Dad laughs. "Nah, kid's more like his mom. A little soft, but a couple months in this job, he'll harden up."

Dorian rolls her eyes at him, making me instantly like her. "Not everyone around here is hard and we do just fine."

Still chuckling, Dad walks closer and clutches her shoulder. "Dorian here is married to a judge. You'll want to get in good with her." He winks at me in that devious way of his. Like, get into her pants and you're golden.

Gritting my teeth, I ignore my father. She steps back, out of his reach, and shakes her head. "Judge Rowe. I'm sure you'll see him around in court. He's a hardass who has a soft spot for kids." She smiles as she regards the many frames. In one, she's holding a baby and the others, there are two young women around my age or so. "So, you'll be officing beside me? Have you met Dane yet?"

We met, and then an hour later, I had his dick in my mouth. I suppose you could say we've met.

"I have." I force a smile.

"Dane's the best thing about this place," she says, grinning. "He's my husband's best friend."

Dad faux pouts. "I thought I was the best thing about this place."

God, Dad's flirting is so fucking pathetic. I've never witnessed it in his environment before. Usually, I just see the results of said flirting when he's sneaking one out of the house.

Dorian laughs at him. "Go away, Stratton. Your cologne is giving me a headache."

He grunts, but motions for me to follow him.

"Nice to meet you," I tell her as we exit.

"My pleasure," she says, her tone once again friendly for me.

At least I know she's immune to my dad's sick charm.

Dad shows me around to a few more people, including my assistant with a giant pair of tits and the biggest 'fuck me' lips I've ever seen, before he leaves me be in my office. Susan aka Tits & Lips has come into my office no less than fifteen times to bend over the front of my desk to hand me files.

I should put her out of her misery and tell her I'm gay, but then, I don't know how that would spread through the office. And, if anything, I'm not ready to divulge that to a building full of suits. Not to mention, I can't have Dad breathing down the back of my neck, warning me to stay away from Dane.

Dane is my problem to deal with.

I pick through a few files but settle on the one that is most time-sensitive. Last semester, in college, I interned at a firm not far from here. When college ended, though, Dad made sure to snag me a better job than the other firm. This one pays a helluva lot more.

Malachi and Xavier Bryant. Seven and five years old. Multiple child abuse accounts stemming from damn near birth. First, a lot of the shit attached to their names was because of their mother, Ellen.

Heroine-addict who neglected her kids. One report shows they were left in the car outside an apartment building overnight. In between her neglect charges were hospitalizations of both her and the kids from her husband, Jayson. Jayson went on to kill her, after beating the shit out of her one too many times when the kids were just five and three. He spent the next year in prison before he was stabbed to death in an inmate fight. The kids, who had been staying with foster families, were now official wards of the state.

"What the fuck," I grumble, as I flip through some gruesome pictures that are dated October of this year. Both kids have matching black eyes and the older boy has a split lip. So fucking sad. I read on to learn that there's a case against the most recent foster home, where the woman, Juanita Aikens, physically abused not only these two, but a couple others, including a seventeen-year-old girl named Jenna and a two-year-old girl named Cora. Enzo Tauber is the social worker on not only the boys' case but also each one of the girls.

I knew from my internship that some cases would be sad. I just didn't expect to get one right out of the gate. My phone buzzes and I glance at the clock on my old-ass computer. Lunchtime.

Dane: I'm back from court. The black Porsche Cayenne double parked out front is mine. Move your ass, Stratton.

All depressing thoughts about my case bleed away as I rise from my chair and stand. I shouldn't be going off to lunch with my boss, considering his dick was in my ass just this morning, but *because* his dick was in my ass has me eager to see him. So much for staying away.

Susan purses her lips at me as I leave in a way surely meant to be seductive but comes off as desperate and fish-like. I wave to her and grumble out that I'm headed to lunch. My dad isn't in his office, thank fuck.

It isn't until I'm out of the office and being pelted by sleet that I let out a relieved breath. The air clouds white around my face and a shiver runs through me. I knew it was most likely going to snow, and yet I'd been so on fire from my weekend with Dane that I opted for no coat. I'm kind of wishing I'd grabbed it after all. I rush over to the sleek Porsche with black wheels and dark tinted windows. When I open the passenger side door, his scent rushes out, enveloping me. Warms me straight to my dick.

"Hey," I grunt out as I climb inside and shut the

door behind me. It's hot in the vehicle and my glasses fog up. I yank them off and turn my attention toward Dane.

Fuck, he's hot.

His suit is hidden beneath a long, black dress coat and he wears black leather gloves. The power of his masculine fingers strains against the material. My cock twitches with a fantasy of one of those gloved hands around my throat as he fucks me in his backseat.

"Where's your coat?" he demands, his brow hitching up.

"I was hot this morning." I shrug, but pin him with a firm stare.

A smug grin tugs on his lips at one side, making me ache to fucking kiss him again. "Maybe I'll have to warm you up again."

My dick, eager for his suggestion, is hard and fully erect in my slacks. But, despite its willingness to play, I can't. It's not that I'm afraid for people to find out I'm sleeping with the managing partner, it's what happens when I fuck it up.

I will fuck it up.

I always do.

There's a reason why I don't do relationships.

Every one I've attempted has failed miserably. The guy gets attached and I become detached. It's like, the more into me they are, the more I want to bail. It will happen with Dane and me. He's already admitted he's not a fuck-and-run type of guy.

Well, he fucked the wrong guy—because *I* run, dammit.

"Everything okay?" he asks as he pulls onto the road.

My glasses have lost their fog, so I slide them back on and give him a clipped nod. "Just overwhelmed by first day shit. Nothing I can't handle though."

"Susan said you had the *Golden versus Elliot* case. It's one of the ones I passed off to you. If you need assistance, let me know."

Guilt scratches at my insides. Why does he have to be so fucking nice? It makes pushing him away that much harder.

"Seems easy enough. We dealt with civil cases like that all the time at Becker, Goins, and Stiller. That's where I interned at," I say lamely. Apparently, I can fuck this guy with no problems but carrying on a normal conversation has me flustered.

"Good firm," he says, and then grins my way. "Ours is better. Have you met Miller yet?"

"Dad never took me to the other side of the office, and then I dove straight into work. Is he an attorney too?"

He laughs. "No, he's a motherfucking shark. Biggest asshole on the damn planet since his wife left him. But he's a good guy. If you ever need any case help, come to me or Miller. Your dad…" He trails off. "No offense, but there are better lawyers at our firm who can help."

I smirk. "None taken. Don't tell Dad that, though. I'm pretty sure he thinks he's God's gift to the justice system." I grow serious for a moment. "How familiar are you with the Bryant case?"

He winces and frowns. "The abused kids?"

"Yeah."

"I've been briefed on it but that's really Miller's expertise."

"Who does that to their kids?" I ask, my voice hollow. "Who does that to kids in general?"

"Sick fucks," he grunts. "I see a lot of that shit with my divorce cases where custody battles ensue. There are a lot of assholes who hurt kids out there. Not just physically, but emotionally too."

My mind drifts to when I was thirteen. The way my dad had his hands all over Fawna from next door.

I'd stared, horrified that it was some pretty woman who wasn't my mother. And the slew of insults, mainly calling me a prying sonofabitch, haunt me to this day. If anyone knows about parents emotionally fucking up their kids, it's me. My dad started that day and has gotten a million times worse over the years. I don't even want to think about the day I'd told him I was gay. Absently, I rub my jaw that still aches from time to time, and that's been eight years now.

"Still in the mood for burgers?" Dane grunts as we park in front of a hole-in-the-wall dive.

"Yep."

"Hope you're hungry for a pretty side of dick," he says with a wicked grin.

I gape at him, confused by his words.

"Miller is joining us for lunch. Don't let him dazzle you with his good looks. He's the grumpiest motherfucker I know." He chuckles. "And I know a lot of grumpy motherfuckers."

Dane

Nick follows silently behind me into the dark restaurant that reeks of stale cigarette smoke and onions. The smell clings to your clothes and I'll have to have my coat dry cleaned, but it's worth it for the burgers. Best in this damn town.

I steal a glance over my shoulder at Nick. His brows are furled as he broods. I'm realizing he had no idea who I was when he invited me to his room this weekend and it's majorly fucking with his head. As much as it's a bad idea to want him because of our positions, I can't help the fact that he makes my dick hard, just from looking at him. He looks handsome as hell in those glasses of his. His red eyes are from lack of sleep and not from getting high, unfortunately. If it wasn't a work day and we were anywhere but here, I'd tell him to smoke a blunt and chill the fuck out. I'm learning quickly there are two Nicks. The one from this weekend—the real one—and this closed off version he reserves for everyone else.

Someone whistles from the back, stealing my attention, and I see August snapping his fingers at us from a high-backed booth. Lunch with two broody assholes. Awesome. I slide into the booth across from August and scoot over to allow room for Nick. He sits beside me, stiff and rippling with intensity.

"Nick, meet my asshole friend, August Miller. Miller, meet Nick Stratton," I introduce.

August's green eyes narrow as he scrutinizes the man beside me. Neither man offers the other his hand, instead nodding. I guess it'll be one of those lunches where I do all the damn talking.

"Chandler's son?" August finally asks, his dark brown eyebrow lifting. He hates Chandler. But August hates everyone, so that's nothing new.

"Yep," Nick grits out.

August's eyes sear into mine and they flicker much like a shark's would in bloody water. Hungry for a bite. He wants to nibble and pick at this new fish in our water because that's what he does. Not because he's attracted to him, but because he wants to watch him squirm. Sadistic bastard. It's what makes him a valuable attorney in the courtroom. Unfortunately, he'll have to stick with eating a goddamned burger. Nick's mine to bite.

I give August a slight shake to the head—meaning, *don't fuck with him*. August is one of the few people who knows of my past curiosity of men. I'd rambled that tidbit of information one day over one too many drinks as I bitched about Janice. I'm sure he can interpret the silent claim I'm staking over Nick.

His lips twitch on one side. I've long admired this handsome-as-shit friend of mine, but that's all. He was straight as an arrow. I was married. It wasn't anything worth pursuing. Now that I have Nick beside me, I realize I much prefer Nick's lips. With his thigh brushing against mine, jolts of need are surging through me. August, no matter how fucking hot, never invoked such a response from me. Hell, Janice never did either.

"Hmmm," is all August says after a moment. "You going to Felix's benefit party Friday?"

I groan. We all fucking hate Felix Mullins, but sometimes you do shit you don't want to do, like office Christmas parties and women and political ass kissing. Felix is a district attorney campaigning for senator. It's always good to have a public official up your sleeve in case you ever need any favors. In my line of work, you always need favors. "Do we have to?"

August smirks. "We don't, but every other asshole in the city will be there. Might be kind of obvious if we don't show up."

We're interrupted by an older woman who takes our order. Nick is unusually quiet so I nudge him with my shoulder. "Want to come with us?"

He turns and our faces are too close. So close, I could easily lean forward and kiss his plump lips. Just thinking about them has my eyes dropping their way.

"Not really," Nick grumbles. "Unless I have to."

I bite back a laugh. His smartass remark is one I remember from this weekend and am eager to see more of it. "You have to. I'm the boss. I make the rules."

His gaze darkens, but then he pulls his stare away to excuse himself to the restroom. When I look at August, he's actually grinning. Like a wily coyote, but still smiling. Freaky bastard.

"You're fucking the kid." His nostrils flare as his grin grows wider.

I crack my neck, glance out at the thickening dusting of snow outside, before regarding him with an even expression. "Whatever, man."

"I knew it. I had an assumption when you brought in a walking, talking Hollister-looking model, but damn, does it feel good to be right."

The waitress brings us our beers and a basket of onion rings.

I chug down half my beer in one gulp before shrugging at him. "I'm doing what I want for a change."

He nods. "Not judging."

Letting out a heavy sigh, I lean forward, feeling like a gossipy girl. "I don't know what I'm fucking doing, August. I met him at the hotel bar Friday night at the Christmas party and discovered he works for me on Monday." I rub at the tension in the back of my neck. "We just really hit it off."

August smirks. "By hit it off, you mean you fucked the good-looking kid all weekend. Got a taste for a man and decided you'd have the whole damn meal?"

Shaking my head, I flip him off. "Thanks for oversimplifying the most unusual but fucking awesome time in my life. Great friend you are."

He snorts. "I'm not the friend who strokes your ego and strokes your cock. That's what Max is for."

I sip my beer and can't help but smile at his stupid ass. "You know what happened the last time I tried a move on Max."

And he does. That drunken night, I spilled to August about how my best friend broke my fucking heart when he nearly broke my face.

"Max?" Nick asks, as he slides into the booth beside me.

"Judge Rowe," August blurts out like a fucking teenage girl. "You know him?"

Nick's brown eyes dart to mine. "I met his wife earlier today."

"Tell us more," August urges me, wickedness gleaming in his green eyes. I'll get his ass back later for this.

"Back when we were in college, I thought Max might be into me like I was into him. We were drunk, I tried to kiss him, he tried to kill me. After he nearly knocked my ass out, we got over it, and it never happened again. He's still my best friend," I explain, irritated at August for bringing it up.

"What a dick," Nick grunts out, his gaze softening slightly.

"Rowe is a good guy," I defend. "He just doesn't swing that way. It was my mistake. I was testing out my sexuality, and apparently testing it out on your heterosexual best friend was a bad idea."

"He shouldn't have hit you, though," Nick argues, his brown eyes turning sharp.

"If Max were my best friend, I'd have knocked him back in the fucking skull," August offers, his own bitterness bubbling up with his words.

Of course these two knuckleheads would agree on this. A best friend bashing party. Fucking wonderful. But, considering August hates everyone and is choosing to side with my guy, I consider this a win in some way. My grin must give me away because August rolls his eyes.

"Nick took the Bryant case. I told him to come to you if he has any problems or questions," I say, changing the subject.

The waitress delivers our burgers and we spend the next half hour discussing the case. August looks thirsty for blood whereas Nick looks like he might throw up. Sometimes these cases wear you down. I thought handling divorces would be less stressful, but it's not any easier than the rest. Almost always, my job consists of me stepping between two squabbling people dead set on destroying each other, and urging them to settle on something fairly. It's never that simple.

"I researched the new home they'd been placed in," Nick says, after polishing off his burger. "It didn't yield much results."

"Did you talk to Enzo? He's the case worker on that one, right?" August asks.

Nick shakes his head. "Not yet, but I'm going to reach out to him."

I don't remind Nick that his job is to prosecute the foster mom who abused those children. Their safety and whereabouts isn't attorney privilege information. His job is to defend the innocent and bring the hammer down on the guilty.

"Well, I gotta get the hell out of here," August says. "I have a mountain of shit to do and need to leave by three." He pulls out some cash and I wave it off.

"I've got lunch. But your surly ass better show up for the New Years party in a few weeks. What the hell was so much more important than our office Christmas party?" I demand as I hand the waitress my card.

"Everything," August says with a shrug. "I had something better to do."

"Invite her," I say, grinning. "Maybe you'll actually come."

Nick snorts.

"Oh, I'll be coming all right," August retorts.

"Whatever. Just make sure you show up or I'll come find your ass. See you around the office," I call out.

He's already stalking out of the restaurant, waving over his shoulder.

"Asshole," I grumble.

Nick chuckles. "And you're friends with him. What does that say about you?"

I nudge him with my shoulder. "Maybe I like taking in the mean strays. I have a soft spot for growly biters, it would seem."

His brown eyes darken. "You make this really damn hard to fight," he complains.

Sliding my palm over his thigh, I grip his thick muscle through his slacks. "Nobody's asking you to resist."

He frowns, turning his head from me. I lean in and nip at his throat. A low groan rumbles from him and his face snaps back to meet mine. Since he's feeling torn, I make the move. I lean forward until our lips meet. I kiss him firmly and stake my claim. With a sigh, he gives in, opening his mouth for me. Our tongues lash at each other as if they are at war. Just like in the courtroom, I prefer to win.

And I will win this moody motherfucker over.

This time, I drive into the parking garage since I have more work to do. I pull into a spot and Nick lets out a low whistle.

"Who the fuck is compensating for a small dick?" he asks as he admires the cherry red and chrome Jaguar F-Type.

"August, and he's got a big dick. It's his present to himself for having to deal with his bitch ex-wife's cheating."

"You've seen his dick?" he challenges, a smirk on his lips that are still red from our heated kiss in the restaurant.

"Nah, but man, have I heard stories around the office."

He smiles but then wipes it away as he reaches for the car door handle. I grip his thigh, stopping him from leaving.

"This past weekend was the best of my life," I admit, my voice husky. "And I'm not ready for it to end."

Nick scowls and it makes me want to kiss that pissy look right off his face. "We can't work. You know this."

"It's not the eighties anymore, man. Guys fuck

each other. It's a thing. I thought I'd be the one with issues here, but you're suddenly embarrassed about what we have going on?" I ask, hating the way my stomach tightens with nerves.

His gaze hardens. "We fucked over the weekend. That's the only thing we have going on."

The biting sting of rejection is all that's left long after he exits my car. But instead of letting his grumpy ass push me away so easily, I text him my address and then a note to go along with it.

Me: When you get tired of lying to yourself, here's where I'll be.

He doesn't respond.

SEVEN

Nick

A week later...

I thought avoiding Dane would be difficult. That maybe he'd pressure me and pry. He did nothing like that. Just let me settle in my job and flashed me the occasional smoldering grin. So many days, I wanted to take him up on that offer. Drive over to his house and fuck his brains out.

But each day, long after dark, I'd pack my messenger bag full of files and take my not-so-merry ass home. Home to where I still live with my parents and sister. It's another thing held high over my head. Dad would pay for college, give me a car, and keep my checking account cushy. All I had to do was follow his plan.

Now, I'm so fucking tired of his plan, I want to

scream. I spent my lunch hour looking for apartments because there's no way I can spend another minute at home watching Mom text all night with her secret boyfriend, or my dad strut around like he's the best father in the world all the time, knowing he's already fucked half that firm. Even Christina is fake. Mom had a hand in her beauty pageant days, then her cheerleading days, and now her modeling days. Christina has been molded into perfection, just like their eldest son.

I need something real.

Like him.

I skipped the political benefit he wanted me to go to. I figured it was a bad idea. A few drinks into me and I'd end up in his bed again. Instead, I sat at home and got high.

"Bubs?" Christina calls out when I walk in the house.

I find her sitting at the bar in the kitchen, frowning at her phone. "What's up?"

"It's frozen." My sister, with her big brown eyes and silky brown hair, was once sweet and curious. Now, she's always so stiff and forced. She'll be a plastic Barbie just like Mom in no time. Fucking sad, really.

"Let me see it," I grunt, reaching out for her

precious lifeline that never leaves her hand.

"I'm sure it's just hung up and it'll start working again." Her cheeks turn pink as she mashes some buttons.

"Did you try restarting it?"

Her lip curls up. "I am right in the middle of editing my photo for Instagram. I'll lose the changes. I can't restart it."

"Restart it."

"No."

"Chris, dammit, restart the phone."

"No."

Just like when we were younger, I use my size to my advantage. I snag her phone and hold it up in the air so I can restart it. She squeals and swipes the air, trying to get it. Before the screen goes dark, I get a glimpse of a text from Eli.

"Who's Eli?" I ask as the phone restarts.

Her cheeks blaze red. "None of your business, asshole."

I laugh and slap her phone back into her palm. "Where's Mom?"

"Shopping," she says absently as she stares at her screen.

"Hmmm," I rumble. "I'm moving out."

She doesn't look up but she does smile. For her camera. My sister holds out her arm and snaps a pic. Jesus, kids these days are obsessed with their phones.

"Did you hear me?"

She nods and taps away, completely not hearing what I'm saying.

"Right, you're welcome for fixing your phone." I stalk out of the kitchen and walk through our home. It's cold and too clean. Disturbingly so. Mom can't handle dust. Says she's allergic, although she's never proven as much. Our house cleaner, Lin, comes three times a week and Mom still bitches about it being dusty.

Even my room must remain immaculate. Sterile gray walls. Always freshly vacuumed carpets. Nothing out of place.

Sure enough, when I push into my room, the socks I'd left on the floor are gone. The change on my dresser has been removed. The laptop I'd been working on, that was strewn across the floor, has been placed neatly in a box and tucked under a chair.

I need to get the fuck out of here.

With a heavy sigh, I drop my messenger bag on the floor and strip along the way to the shower. Lin will be disappointed at having to clean up after me.

Right now, I don't care. I turn on the hot shower and then step inside. And just like every night this week, I think of him.

Dane Alexander.

Too fucking hot for his own good.

Bitterness roils in my stomach. Had I just gone off and done what I'd wanted to for college, maybe I'd still have met him through Dad. I could have dated him like normal. I'm sure we'd still have hit it off, no matter where we met.

But that didn't happen.

I met the most untouchable guy I could.

Dark grayish-blue eyes. Full lips. Just enough facial hair to scratch my lips when we kiss but not enough to hold onto. I groan as my dick aches for attention. Stroke after stroke, I imagine myself pumping into his tight virgin ass. He'd felt amazing. And then, when he ravaged me, he was feral and uncontained. I loved the way he lost himself inside me. Despite what I'd told him, that I prefer to do the fucking, I actually really enjoyed being on the receiving end.

Cum jets out of me suddenly as I let out a sharp hiss of air. My climax is good but the lingering burn in my gut remains. It's not just about the sex. It's about the conversation and how that big fucker liked to cuddle. Just wrapped his possessive arm around me and hugged me to him.

I could really use a fucking hug right now.

Instead of feeling sorry for myself, I dry off and dress in a pair of sweats. I lounge on my bed as I pour through the Bryant file. I'd spoken to Enzo. At least their caseworker was adamant about placing them someplace safer this time—he'd been infuriated. That made two of us. I was glad that he was feeding me information about the kids. Something about those two made me feel so fucking sorry for them.

I guess I have a soft spot for kids too, like Judge Rowe.

Irritation boils in my stomach. The same judge who punched his best friend for making a move. If I ever meet this guy, I can't say I'll be sucking up to him like Dad wants. I'll probably want to kick his ass.

I'm lost in my notes when my bedroom door flings open. Dad stumbles in, drunk. More and more after work, he gets plastered. Comes home with lipstick on his collar, stinking of pussy, and acts like a complete asshole. Thank God Christina is never around for this shit. It's like he saves it all for his son.

"What?" I bark out.

He glowers. "Don't you *what* me, boy."

I give him a hard stare. "Need something, dear father?" I sneer, my voice condescendingly sweet.

He bumps into my end table and sends the lamp thumping to the carpet. Then, his hands are on my shoulders, yanking me out of the bed.

"What the fuck?" I roar, shoving him from me.

His drunk ass slams against the wall. Bloodshot eyes meet mine as he snarls, "I told you not to embarrass me."

"I always seem to embarrass you, Dad. What did I do this time?" I mock.

"Missy said she saw you flirting at the party with Dane. Then, Susan said you went to lunch with him last week. Are you…" Disgust makes him shudder. "Are you fucking him?"

"No," I snap. "Not that it's any of your business who I fuck."

"It *is* my business," he roars. "My reputation is on the line. My whore son is ruining everything!"

I growl as I stalk over to him. "You're calling *me* the whore? You fuck anyone who isn't Mom!"

Crack!

His right hook, just like the last time we fought two months ago, comes out of nowhere. My head snaps to the side as pain radiates across my face. That motherfucker. I hold back because I don't know what he'd do. I certainly don't need him telling my mom and sister I kicked his ass. No telling what kind of story he'd spin.

"Get out of my room," I hiss, rubbing my jaw.

Fury radiates from him. "No, you cock-sucking princess, you get out of my house. Handout time is over."

My nostrils flare as anger overwhelms me. "Gladly, motherfucker."

He picks up the remote control on the dresser and throws it at me. It hits me in the mouth. Pain bursts from my lip as I stare at him in shock. Who is this man? What kind of dick pushes around his kid?

I could push back.

But then it makes me just like him.

I'm *nothing* like that asshole.

Blood rushes from my lip and drips to the floor. Lin will have a helluva time getting the stain out.

"I want you to quit. I don't want to see your fruity ass anymore," Dad mumbles, his words thick and sludgy from being drunk.

"I'll leave, but I'm not quitting," I bite back. "See you around, Chandler."

His face is red. He sends a fist through my wall,

the drywall exploding upon impact. With a jerk, he pulls his hand away and stalks out of the room.

I let out a heavy sigh of relief.

Time to get the fuck out of here.

"Another one, hot stuff?" the bartender asks.

She's cute. Tall and thin. Bright pink hair. I'd fuck her if I were into chicks. But I'm not. I'm into dicks. One in particular.

"Briiing it," I slur out.

Her brow lifts and she smiles. "One more and you're cut off, handsome."

"Babe," I murmur. "Babe."

She wiggles her ass as she makes the drink. "Yeah, handsome?"

"I'm Nick. Nick is into dicks. I'd fuck you if I were into chicks. Nick isn't into chicks. Dicks." I scratch my jaw and nearly fall off the stool. "Get it?"

She snorts with laughter as she sets down a shot. "Last one."

"You're bossy. Like Dane. Dane is bossy."

"Dane's your 'dick'?"

I nod like a bobblehead and then knock back

my shot. She takes my phone from me and scrolls through it. I watch her, my eyes drooping. Then, she sets it back down before making another drink.

"My dad's a dick," I reveal. "Not a good dick. An asshole dick."

She laughs. "Isn't everyone's dad a dick?"

"You got a point there. Most of them are," I murmur.

She sets a glass of ice water down, and I look at it before bringing my gaze up to meet hers.

"Oh no, handsome," she says. "Those puppy dog eyes don't work on me, now that I know we're not hooking up. You get water because your ass is drunk. Drink all this water and I might give you some coffee. Be a good boy."

I flip her off but chuckle. My eyes feel heavy. It's late, on a work night. I should be figuring out where the fuck I'm going after this. Maybe a little nap will clear my head. The bar top is cool against my cheek. From down at the other end of the bar, some guy watches me like I'm pitiful.

Maybe I am.

Fuck.

Hell yeah, I am.

As fucking pitiful as they come.

EIGHT

Dane

"Christmas, Dad."

I groan as I drive. "Fine. I'll be there."

"Mom is bringing a date," she says softly. "Are you going to be okay?"

Stifling a yawn, I shrug. "Honestly, sweetheart, I've never been better. How are you and Stan?"

"We're doing well. It's one of the reasons I wanted you to come over for Christmas," she says, her voice soft and unsure.

Stan is an okay guy. Kind of nerdy. My girl could get someone better but, for some reason, she likes this guy. They've been dating a few years now. Met in college and now live together.

"I'll be there. You know I will."

She sighs. "I know. I know I can always count on you. It's Mom who…" She trails off. "Mom's new guy is kind of an asshole. Don't tell her I said that."

"I'm hard to beat," I tease.

"You're irreplaceable," she agrees. "See you soon, Daddy. Love you."

"Love you too, Mel."

We hang up and I can't wipe the stupid grin off my face. Mel and I are busy with our lives but any time we talk, I feel like we're back to when she was nine, sitting on my lap while we binge-watched *I Love Lucy* reruns. Mel's always been my little sidekick. When she went off to college, though, she grew up on me. Got her own life. It was truly the moment when Janice and I began to fizzle out completely. Without Mel bringing us together, we weren't anything.

I pull into the parking lot of a bar and climb out. The blistery wind is too fucking cold and I rush inside as quick as I can to avoid the elements. The weather says we're about to get pounded with a snowstorm.

Inside the bar, it smells like smoke. And fried cheese. The jukebox is playing some old Led Zeppelin tune. This place is for old men like me.

Not drunk ass young men.

Especially not snoring ones.

"Stop," the pink-haired bartender says, swatting at some guy sitting next to Nick.

He's trying to balance his cup on Nick's head. What a dick. I stalk over their way and the moment the bar patron sees me, he slides off his stool and stumbles away, taking his cup with him.

"You must be the dick," the bartender says, waving.

I frown. "Dane."

"That's the one," she chirps. "I'm Foxxy."

I try not to cringe at that name. "Great, Foxxy. How much do I owe you for his tab?"

She slaps the bill down and I settle it with a wad of cash, making sure to tip her well for texting me from this drunk ass's cell phone.

"Hey," I grunt, running my fingertips through his hair. "Wake up."

He mutters out something unintelligible. Then, he sits up and stares at me. Even with his eyes blood-shot and hooded, drool smeared across his chin, and his lip swollen and split, he's fucking hot.

"What the hell happened to you?" I growl.

He shrugs and nearly falls off the stool. I slip an arm around him and help him to his feet. His body slumps against mine, his fingers clutching my coat.

Speaking of coats…

"Did you bring anything warmer to wear?"

"I'm hot," he slurs. "You make me hot."

People are beginning to stare and normally, I might be a little freaked out to be seen with a man, since this is still all so new to me. But right now, Nick's well-being is my primary concern. The other people here can go fuck themselves.

"Let's get you home," I grumble as I guide him out of the bar.

"I can't go back." His words are sharp and punctuated.

"You're coming home with me."

He looks up at me with the saddest fucking eyes I've ever seen. Once I get to the bottom of why he's like this, I'm going to help him. Whatever has him upset, we'll deal with together. He may have started as a random fuck in a hotel, but that's not what he is to me now.

The snow pelts us and he bitches at it. I bite back a chuckle as I help him into my Porsche. He rests his head against the headrest and starts snoring before I have him buckled in. Once I'm in the driver's seat and have the car started, I stare at him. Sleeping, he looks just like he did the weekend we met. Since then, he's been tense as fuck at the office. I didn't want to push him since he's clearly uncomfortable with my being his boss, but I'm tired of sitting back and watching him be so unhappy. He needs someone to talk to. I want to be that someone.

I drive us home and for a brief moment consider going to my cabin by the lake. If we weren't threatened by a damn near blizzard, it'd be the perfect place to get him away, and for him to unwind. But, for now, he'll have to settle for my house. It's the same one Mel grew up in. The same one where I spent all those years with my wife. She left and got a fancy loft, in August's building of all places. It's more to her speed. Sleek, over-the-top expensive, with a spa on the bottom floor. I'm just glad to get her out of my house.

I pull into the garage and my stomach grumbles. I was working late when I got the text about Nick. Missed dinner too. He's heavy as hell passed out, and I nearly drop his ass a few times getting him inside. Once we step into the warm kitchen, he wakes up and stands on his own two feet.

"Where are we?" he murmurs.

I help him into the living room and onto the sofa. "My house. You hungry?"

He nods and rubs his eyes with the heels of his

hands. I leave him be to shed my coat and search for something to cook. It's not my first choice, but I settle for popping a frozen lasagna in the oven. Since we have to wait an hour for it to cook, I brew a pot of coffee to sober Nick up. Once I've made us both a cup, I walk back into the living room.

He's kicked off his shoes and wrapped up in Mel's favorite blanket for when she visits. It's pulled over the top of his head, and right now, he looks a lot younger than his twenty-five years. Instead of wanting to jump his bones, I want to fix whatever is making him look so small and lost.

I hand him his mug and set mine down on the coffee table. "I'm going to change. I'll be right back. Bathroom is first door on the right in the hallway. Make yourself at home."

Quickly, I changed out of my suit and settle for a pair of dark gray sweats and a long-sleeved white T-shirt. Since I'm still cold as fuck, I pull on my old man slippers Mel got for me last Christmas. At the time, I'd thanked her but thought hell no would I be caught dead wearing Sherpa-lined house shoes. But my girl knows me. They're comfortable and I love them.

"You have a lot of pictures," Nick says when I

enter the room.

I glance around the living room. Half of them are missing. Janice took as many as she could of Mel. I had to fight her over some of them. All that's left are ones of my daughter and I, and a few of just Mel.

"Yeah," I agree and plop down beside him. "Are we going to discuss why your lip is split and how come you're shitfaced on a weeknight?"

He sips his coffee. "My dad's an asshole."

"Your dad hit you?" I grit my teeth together.

His brown eyes sweep my way and he frowns, giving me a slight nod. Fuck if he doesn't look like he's about to cry.

"Did you hit him back?" I growl.

His head shakes and he drinks another sip of his coffee. "Nah. He's my dad."

"And you're his son," I hiss, fury bubbling as hot inside me as the cup of coffee in my grip.

When he doesn't reply, I sip some of my coffee before setting it down on the coffee table. Reaching over, I clutch his shoulder. "It's not okay for him to hit you," I say as calmly as I can. "I'm sorry."

He blinks at me several times before darting his gaze away. "Mel's pretty."

Following his stare, I find my daughter smiling

back at me from her high school senior picture hanging over the fireplace. "She takes after her mom."

At this, he snorts. "She has the same intense stormy gray eyes you have."

"I guess she has my personality too," I say with a chuckle. "Mel's determined."

He reaches forward to set his mug down on the table. "I'm sorry I started something I couldn't finish."

I take his hand in mine and my stomach does a flop when he doesn't pull it away. Whatever it is going on between Nick and I since the day we locked eyes in that bar hasn't shown any signs of stopping, no matter what he tries to do to push me away. This all feels backwards—the fucking first and then the feelings. But I don't care. Right now, holding his hand as he unloads his problems feels good. Better than good.

"Why can't we finish it?" I ask, squeezing his hand.

"My dad…" He trails off and winces. "I'm a fucking embarrassment to him."

I release his hand to pull him to me. At first, he's stiff in my embrace and then he relaxes, clinging to me like I've just pulled him from a churning ocean. "Listen to me, Nick. Your dad is a piece of shit. End of story. He should feel lucky to have a son like you. I'm sorry that he hit you and makes you feel like you're unworthy of his love. But fuck him, babe. Fuck him, because his opinion doesn't matter. You're an intelligent, hard-working guy who's nice to people. Your dad isn't even a quarter of the man you are."

He pulls slightly away and his brown eyes sear into mine. "I have daddy issues," he snorts. Then, his drunk ass plucks at my whiskers on my face. "You think that's why I like this salt-and-pepper shit? Because I get some sort of sick satisfaction from it?"

I grip his wrist and pull his hand away. "I'm not your dad, Nick. You don't fuck me because I remind you of him. You fuck me because we're good together. And you're going to continue to fuck me because you feel that insane burning inside your chest like I do. Like you can't get enough.

"It's been hell having to watch you walk around the office with your sexy-as-fuck pouty face, and not drag you into my office. I've given you your space because for some crazy ass reason, you think we need to stay away from each other. But I'm done. I'm done waiting around for you to wise up. Seems like you're never going to get it through your thick skull that you're able to get what you want in this life. Nobody else dictates you. Only you." Leaning forward, I rest my forehead against his. "And I want you. I know you want me back too."

His lips crash to mine as he pounces on me, pushing me back against the cushions. Our mouths part and his tongue that tastes like liquor and coffee swipes over mine. My dick is hard as stone from a simple kiss and by the way he rubs against me, I can tell he's hard too. His hands are desperate to touch me everywhere as he devours me. I slide my palms to his toned ass and squeeze, pulling his ass cheeks apart. He moans into my mouth, making me even more hungry for him.

"Dane," he groans against my mouth. "I tried to stay away but I don't want to."

"Then don't."

He bites on my bottom lip and tugs before releasing it. "You don't understand. It's not just about my dad. It's about me. I'm not this relationship guy you're looking for. You've seen what kind of family I come from."

His lips hover over mine as he stares at me. Those deep brown eyes implore me to understand. But all I see is his desperate need to be accepted. To be loved and adored and fucking cared for. Well, this stubborn ass came to the right place. I've been looking for the same thing for twenty-six long years.

"You think you'll get involved and then get bored?" My brows furrow together as I admire his handsome face. His hair has lost the gel and hangs over his forehead into his eyes. A rosy blush spread over his cheeks from our fevered kiss. But it's those lips I crave. Even with the split lip, looking angry and tender. I want to lick it until it heals. I want to lick *him* until his heart heals.

"It's what I do," he rasps out, shame flickering in his eyes.

"Because you hadn't met me yet," I tell him confidently. "I'm not stupid, Nick. There's something tethering us together. It's as tangible as our physical connection. You have things I need and I have things you need. Let's give them to each other. Let's take from each other. Be a greedy bastard with me."

He smiles, crooked, and it's fucking adorable. "I like taking from you."

"You took my virginity," I say with a smirk.

A chuckle rumbles from him. "Tightest ass I've ever been in. What kind of glutes exercises are you doing? I'd say you're doing them wrong, but hell, I'm not complaining."

"Smartass." I run my fingers through his unruly

hair and grow serious again. "Stay with me until you get back on your feet. If you decide you want to move on, then I won't hold it against you. But if things work out…" I kiss his supple mouth. "Let it, Nick. Just fucking let it."

I don't get a response.

Just his crushing kiss. Hard enough I taste blood from his injured lip. I think it's his promise to try.

That's all I'm asking.

NINE

Nick

After a two heaping plates of lasagna and a half a pot of coffee, my buzz is nearly gone. The cold reality of my situation settles heavily in my gut. It's snowing hard outside and I'm nursing yet another cup of coffee while Dane cleans up the kitchen. He's so happy in his environment. His house is warm and cozy. Everywhere you turn, there's something that's family oriented. Something that indicates this house has been well-lived in and filled with love over the years.

Dane walks over to the back door and stares outside. His hands are on his tapered hips and I get a nice view of his ass in his sweatpants. Earlier, we'd kissed until I just about came in my pants like a fucking teenager. We didn't make it much further because dinner was ready.

But now…

Now, I want to get this man naked.

To turn off my mind and let my body go.

Just like that weekend we met. That weekend was bliss. One of the best I've had in ages. And with every passing second in Dane's house, I can feel the tension bleeding from my shoulders.

"I doubt we're going anywhere tomorrow. It's coming down too heavy," he says, his back still to me. His T-shirt is molded to his frame and I admire his physique. My mouth waters, and I'm desperate to peel his shirt off and run my palms down the muscles on his back. He turns toward me and I rake my gaze down to his cock. He's not hard at the moment but even flaccid, his cock is thick and hangs heavy. The bulge in his sweatpants makes my dick hard.

"I like your sweatpants," I admit with a half grin.

He smirks and drags his stormy eyes along my front, settling his stare on my cock that strains against the material. "I like yours too."

I rise from my chair and cross my arms over my chest. "What now?"

"Now we shower. I miss seeing your naked body." His grin is devilish and my cock twitches.

"Lead the way, old man."

He chuckles and saunters past me. "Old man," he grumbles. "You'll never let that go, will you?"

"Never," I tell him with a laugh.

I follow him down the hallway to a bedroom at the end. It's masculine and the décor looks newer. I'm guessing when his wife split, she took a lot from here. He pulls off his T-shirt and I'm graced with looking at his impressive back. I watch him disappear into the bathroom and then the shower starts. When he returns, he's naked and stroking his hard dick with a devious glint in his eyes.

"Time to get wet," he says.

I rip away my shirt and then shed the rest of my clothes on the way to the bathroom. He stands in the doorway, blocking my path. When I get near him, he grabs my hips and pulls me to him so our stomachs are pressed together. Our erections are like stone smashed between us. His palms squeeze my ass cheeks as he tilts his head, seeking a kiss from me. I grip his rear end too and return the kiss with all the passion I can muster. With Dane, passion comes easy. It's like my mind shuts off with him and I can just… be.

"You drive me crazy," I groan against his lips. "So

fucking crazy."

"You deserve it for the hell you put me through this week," he complains. "You want to know how hard it was to not go into your office, lock the door, and force you to your knees to take my cock in your pouty mouth?"

My dick thumps against him. "You're the one who still needs to learn how to suck dick."

"I've been looking forward to that lesson all week," he rumbles. "You've been a prickly bastard and I've been patient. I'm no longer patient, Nick. Tonight, I'm going to swallow this big dick of yours."

I'm about to shove him down to his knees to keep his smart mouth busy, but then he's pulling me into the shower. I want to turn him around and fuck him, but he has other plans in mind. In a teasing manner, he begins soaping my body down. His strong hands are gentle as he strokes over my most sensitive areas. He makes sure to avoid my dick and it practically weeps from neglect. Our eyes are locked in a heated battle, neither of us willing to back down.

"You're a walking dream come true," he murmurs, once again teasing me on my lower stomach. "You know that, right?"

I snort. "Why?"

He shakes his head, flashing me a wicked smile. "Surely you've seen a mirror, asshole. You're fine as fuck. This body…" He lets out a low whistle. "Turns me the hell on." Then, he smirks. "Plus, you've got a pretty face."

"A pretty face?" I laugh and shake my head at him. "Fuck you."

Finally, his hand grips my aching dick. "Soon, pouty, soon."

"Pouty." I flip him off but he just grins. "I am not pouty."

His roar of laughter echoes off the walls. "Careful, Pinocchio. That nose of yours is going to grow as long as your dick."

"I'm not a liar. And I'm not pouty."

Smirking, he hands me the soap. "Don't drop it."

"You're an asshole."

"One that's been inside yours," he retorts back.

Ignoring him, I set to soaping him down. His dick juts out proudly in front of him, bouncing ever so slightly as it begs for attention. *Down, boy.* I tease him like teased me until his smile is gone and he watches me much like a lion would as it stalks its prey.

He's hungry for me.

And I'm about to feed him.

"Rinse off," I command, a smile tugging at my lips.

I love the way his stormy gray eyes turn darker, as though it turns him on when I order him around. For a bossy fucker, he sure likes the role reversal. We rinse off and when we're done, he shuts off the water and grabs us some towels. He's quiet as he waits for what's next.

"Dry off and lie on the bed. I want your head hanging off and prone to me." I flash him a deviant grin. "I'm about to skull-fuck your sexy face."

Instead of giving me lip, he saunters away. I watch the globes of his ass tense and tighten with each step he takes. God, he's so fucking hot.

I follow after him because he's mine.

I follow after him because he wants me to take.

I follow him because I want to follow after him like nobody I've ever been with before.

Dane is different.

I knew it the second I connected with his lonely, gray-eyed stare. I'd been drawn to him and then plugged into him the moment he spoke. His voice tugged at parts of my insides I didn't know existed. Sensual ones. Unfamiliar ones. Happy ones. I just wanted to keep him talking so that burning in my chest would keep blazing away. And for that entire weekend, it did. He kept me on fire in more ways than one. This past week, avoiding him, has been hell. Now that we're both naked and together, my world feels righted on its axis again.

He's changing me.

And I'm not hating it one single bit.

I just don't like not feeling in control. This feels new and I still worry I'll fuck it all up. The thought of having Dane gone from my life is a twist to the gut. That's a feeling I most certainly hate.

"Like this?" His voice is husky as he watches me, his head upside down, hanging off the side of the bed.

Fuck.

I sear this image into my mind. The image of this Adonis lying on his bed, his full lips parted and waiting, his dick slowly being pulled on by his strong hand.

"You're hot, old man. So hot you're making me lose my mind."

He grins and it looks extra naughty upside down. "I'll take that as a compliment. Now, get over here and feed me your cock, boy."

"Boy?" I prowl over to him, fisting my cock. "Does anything about this look 'boy' to you?"

"I'll need to see it up close to be sure," he murmurs,

eyeing my dick like it's a piece of steak.

I approach him and then slightly slap my dick on his face and against his lips to tease him. "You have to make me believe you want it," I taunt. "Beg for this dick down your throat, D."

"Give me your cock," he orders. Bossy fucker.

"Give me your tongue first."

His hot tongue lashes out to tease the underside of my dick and I let out a sharp hiss of air. Then, he tongues the tip of my erection, tasting the pre-cum that beads there. He groans in pleasure and I bite on my sore bottom lip. Jesus, how I want to shove myself down his throat until he gags.

"I like the taste." His hot breath tickles me as his tongue tentatively searches for more.

Crazy.

He's making me crazy.

"Don't suck dick like a girl, old man. Show me what you like. You know how this is done. You've just been on the wrong side all these years," I tease.

His lips wrap around my girth and I ease into his needy, hot mouth. At first, I let him tongue my dick some as I get it nice and wet. I part my thighs to get a good stance and then begin pushing deeper into his mouth.

"Relax your throat," I instruct. "That's where I want to be."

He hums and grabs my thighs, urging me closer. His hot, wet mouth is torturous. It feels so good—too good. Like I might fucking die of pleasure. I plant a hand on his chest and push against him. The tip of my cock meets resistance at the back of his throat but then he relaxes like instructed. His heated breath from his nose tickles my nuts, sending ripples of pleasure surging through me.

"Fuck, D," I hiss. "Your mouth feels so fucking good."

He groans and the vibrations have me trembling with need. His dick twitches and the tip glistens with pre-cum. If I weren't fucking his face, I'd lick that sexy tip and have a taste of him too.

"I'm going to go deeper," I rumble, my legs shaking with the need to come. "I want to fuck that throat of yours."

His strong fingers dig into my thighs, no doubt bruising me as he urges me to do my worst. With a firm thrust of my hips, I drive into his throat until he gags around me. The vibrations have my eyelids slamming shut in pleasure, but then I pop them back open so I can see him take every long inch of my dick.

Sliding back out, I revel in the way it feels to be inside his mouth. I said he drives me crazy, but the truth is, right now I feel completely sane. One hundred percent homed in on this moment. Nothing can drag me away from the way his tight throat swallows down my cock with each thrust. The sloppy sounds as he breathes and gags and groans are fucking music. I love it. I am greedy for it.

"You should see the way your neck bulges to take my dick, Dane," I hiss. "It's mesmerizing as hell."

He hums in response, causing my legs to tremble again. Slowly, I pull slightly out and then push back in. His Adam's apple is pushed out and I can see the way his throat expands as my dick shoves its way in.

His grip on my thighs becomes commanding as he urges me to go faster or harder. I do both. I lose myself to the sensations. Pure, unfiltered bliss. I fuck his handsome face until my nuts seize up against his nose and I'm losing control. My dick throbs out a massive load deep into his thirsty throat. He swallows against me, sending more ripples of pleasure shooting through me. When I've finally unloaded and my dick is no longer twitching, I slide from him and step away. He rolls over onto his stomach and then sits up on his haunches, a dirty, hungry glint in his wolfish eyes. With the back of his hand, he wipes away the saliva from his face and nods with his head, indicating he wants me closer. I prowl over to him and attack his mouth with a feral kiss.

Salty.

Fucking sweet too.

He tastes too good to be true.

We kiss for some time, with him on his knees and me standing beside the bed until he finally breaks away.

"I'm going to shut down the lights. I'm not done with you, though," he rumbles as he climbs off the bed, his eyes latching on to mine as he walks off.

I smile as I climb into his massive king-sized bed. Once under the covers, I inhale his scent that clings to every surface of this house—a scent I have easily become addicted to. Soon, the lights go off and he climbs into the bed beside me.

His body curls up behind mine and he wraps one of his muscular arms around me. That hard, impressive cock of his is pressed against my ass but he makes no moves to do anything about it.

"*This* feels nice," he rumbles, nuzzling his nose against my hair. "I could get used to *this*."

Me too.

And that scares the shit out of me.

TEN

Dane

He stiffens at my words. When Nick is touching or kissing or fucking, he's the Nick from when we met. But when we talk, he's someone different. This person I don't know very well. I want to find a way to merge them.

"Tell me about your sister," I murmur.

He snorts. "Way to kill a boner, D."

I thrust against him. "Mine's still there. I just want to know more about you."

His body rolls my way and he settles on his back, releasing a heavy sigh. "Why?"

"Because you're naked in my bed. Because you got your ass beat by your dad tonight. Because you're more than just a good fuck to me. I want fuck you, yes, but right now, I want to talk about you."

"Chris is in high school," he grinds out. "She's your typical snotty rich girl. Dad's princess and Mom's puppet. Not much to know."

"You're not close?" I ask, splaying my palm on his chest.

"Nope. It's hard to get close to someone who can't stop taking selfies."

I chuckle. "Sounds like a phase. She'll grow out of it and she'll need her big brother again."

"Yeah," he says softly. "Maybe."

"What do you do for fun?"

"I get high."

We both laugh.

"What do you do for fun that's legal?" I amend.

"In the Stratton house, 'fun' is chiseling away at your future. We study in school. We network. We attend functions and meet the right people. That is the Stratton way." The bitterness in his voice is evident.

"Hmmm…"

"Hmmm? What kind of hmmm was that?"

"It was the kind of hmmm that says we do things differently in the Alexander house."

"Oh yeah?" he asks. "How so?"

"For one, we do fun shit that has nothing to do with our careers."

"You live alone," he says grumpily.

"Not anymore, roomie."

His body tenses once more but rather than let him get all weird about it, I kiss him. I suppose with Nick, I'll have to try a different tactic with him. Pull info out and then distract him with my dick. Pull more info out and then distract him with my dick. Touch and go.

As the kiss heats up and his greedy hand goes for my cock, I pull away. "I have a pool table. I'm not really that good at it but I like it anyway."

"Sounds like loads of fun." His dry tone makes me chuckle.

"Janice would never let me have one," I utter, frowning in the dark. "It was a gift to myself when she left. I put it in her old craft room."

"I'm sorry. She sounds like such a bitch."

"You have no idea."

"So, a pool table, huh?" His tone is playful.

"I have a dart board too," I tell him with a grin. "There's holes all over the fucking wall, but sometimes I hit the target."

"I don't play games," he says. "Well, not anymore."

"You used to?"

He's quiet for a moment. "Yeah. When I was a

kid, my dad was a better dad. We'd play board games a lot. My favorite was Monopoly. Mom would make snacks and we'd play games. When we got tired, we'd watch movies. Christina was too little to play the board games, but she was always happy to eat the snacks." The smile in his voice is wistful.

"I think families are supposed to play games together," I tell him, running my fingers along the grooves of his chest. "I have a whole closetful for when Mel comes over. She'll annihilate anyone in Scrabble."

"She's never played a Stratton," he says with a chuckle.

"I smell a challenge." Then, before I can stop myself, I blurt out my words. "Spend Christmas with me at Mel's."

Again with the stiffness. "I don't know…"

I never thought I'd have to convince my lover to meet my family. I'd assumed when we started this that maybe he'd be the one doing all the convincing since I'm the one coming to terms with my sexuality here. Nonetheless, I have this strong desire for him to meet my daughter.

"Your house doesn't sound like any place you want to be," I urge. "Besides, I'll need someone to help run interference with my soon-to-be ex-wife."

He chuckles. "You're not selling it here, old man. You're going to have to try harder than that."

"Mel makes the best ham," I say.

"Go on…"

"And green bean casserole. So good."

"And…"

"And my sweet little girl goes all out for dessert. There's always, like, five pies to choose from."

"Can I wear my Santa suit?"

"You can wear whatever the hell you want. I just want you there." And that's the damn truth. "I'm nervous as hell showing up with a man. I'm pretty sure Janice will give me all kinds of shit for it too. But Mel will be happy I've brought someone. All I'm saying is, it may not be perfect, but it'll be interesting."

We're quiet for a moment and then he lets out a resigned sigh.

"I'll go. Just know that this is way out of my comfort zone. Families and shit."

"My daughter is amazing," I assure him. "She'll make it fun. Mel is a sweetheart and makes dealing with her mother a breeze. Not all families are cold and distant. Some families are warm and loving."

"I'll believe it when I see it," he grumbles. "Are

you going to fuck me now or what?"

I laugh as I pull away. "Someone's grumpy."

"We've spent half an hour talking about my hard limit."

"I guess I'll have to cheer you up," I tell him happily as I root around in the nightstand drawer for the lube and a condom. Once I'm sheathed and have a coat of lube on my dick, I crawl over to him. "Ready for my cock, pouty?"

He starts to turn away, but I want to kiss him while my dick is inside him. I playfully push his thighs apart and then slide my lubricated cock along the underside of his balls. His breathing is quiet, but then a sharp hiss escapes him as I ease past the tight ring of his asshole. Instead of losing control and fucking him hard like the last time we were together, I slide slowly into him. Torturously slow. Once I'm all the way in, I grip his thigh below the back of his knee and push his leg up to gain further access. He groans in pleasure. I press against his body with mine, seeking out his mouth. In the dark, we meet uncoordinatedly so, but then our lips and tongues do what they've already been conditioned to do.

Kiss like it's the last one we'll ever get.

Hungry. Desperate. Feral.

We devour each other as my hips rock against him. He feels tight around my dick. Every so often, his ass clenches, sending waves of pleasure exploding through me. I'm like a teenager around this guy. He makes me young again. Makes me feel like I can fuck forever—over and over again, despite my age.

I kiss him in a thankful way.

A way that says: thanks for reminding me I'm worthy of something like this.

A way that says: thanks for teaching me it's okay to explore what I want so deeply in my heart.

I don't think I'll ever be able to express how much his hitting on me in that bar that night has fully done for me. It's like I was reborn. Transformed into this man who was meant to follow his desires and attractions, even into unfamiliar territory.

"Dane," he groans, his fingers gripping my hips. "You fuck like you're trying to get inside my goddamned soul."

His husky words send me over the edge. My cock surges with my release, pumping deep inside him, and we both make ragged sounds of pleasure.

"In the relationship world, we don't call this fucking," I tell him simply, as my thrusting slows and I kiss him gently.

It's called making love.

And I've only ever done it once.

My skittish lover won't like that proclamation, though. So, for now, I let our connection—both physical and emotional—blaze to an uncontrollable inferno. And when he's ready, I'll tell him what this is… and why he's not going anywhere.

He belongs here with me.

I knew it, deep down, the moment his sexy ass smiled at me.

I was fucked right then.

Soon, he'll realize he's fucked too.

We'll be fucked together.

"Wake up, sleepyhead."

Nick grunts out something unintelligible and I laugh.

"Come on," I say with a grin, admiring his naked body tangled up in the sheets on my bed. "Coffee's getting cold."

He flips me off but sits up and yawns. I'd love to admire this man's chest while I drink my coffee but I have some crap to work on this morning since I won't be making it into the office. I stride back into the kitchen and sit down at the table, letting my gaze drift out the window.

Snow.

Tons of it too.

So much that there is no way in hell either of us are leaving this house for the next day or two. I smile at this thought. Even if he wants to run away, he can't. I'll wear his ass down when he has nowhere to go.

Ten minutes later, he drags himself into the kitchen and onto a chair. I watch with amusement as he cradles his mug of coffee as though it's the only one he'll ever get. He's wearing his sweats from last night and no shirt, giving me a lovely view of his sculpted shoulders and pecs. I've already showered and dressed for the day, but opted not to wear a suit. Since I won't be going anywhere, I decided to dress in jeans and a waffle-textured black Henley, along with some black boots. Later, I'll need to shovel the driveway for when I do get around to going into the office.

"What're you working on?" he asks.

"Just rescheduling some client appointments. You got some work to do?"

He shrugs. "Everything is in my car."

"You can borrow my laptop if you want."

113

"Yeah," he says, nodding.

I close out what I was working on and hand it over to him. Suddenly, seemingly alert, he furrows his brows and taps away on my computer. *Click* and *tap*. *Click* and *tap*. I watch him as he works and I enjoy my coffee, along with the view. His cheeks are scruffy this morning and his brown hair is a wild mess, but he's hot. No matter what he's wearing or what he's doing, he's hot.

"When was the last time you updated this computer?" he asks, darting his brown eyes my way.

"Who the hell knows. It always asks me to schedule the updates but I never have time. I put it off every time it asks me."

He snorts and shakes his head. "If you'd ever do the updates, your computer wouldn't run like shit."

I frown. I thought it was getting old and was time for a new one. "The updates make it faster?"

He gives me an exasperated look. "Among other things. Everything important saved?"

"Yeah."

"Good."

While he works on it, I fry up some bacon and a couple of eggs for him. I ate at six this morning, but I bet he's starving since it's nearly ten. I fix him a plate and pour us more coffee while he works on my computer.

"Did you sleep well?" I ask, my eyes darting to his lips as he bites into a piece of bacon.

"I slept like a rock."

I smirk. "Yeah, your heavy ass was out. I couldn't have moved you if I'd wanted to." Reaching across the table, I give his hand a squeeze before pulling away. "Not that I wanted to."

His shoulders relax and he gives me a crooked smile. "What are we going to do today? I have no clothes or anything with me."

"Borrow whatever you want. I have extra toothbrushes and anything you might need," I assure him.

While he continues to work, I pull up my phone and check emails. There is one from Max about going out tomorrow night if the roads are cleared, for drinks with his sons-in-law. I like Miles and Drew, so I'm game. I reply back to him that I'll be there, weather permitting, but I'm bringing someone.

"I updated your antivirus. It had expired. Your computer was running like shit, though, because you had a bunch of huge files saved in your C drive. There's a link to the server at the office in a folder on your desktop that'll take you to where you can save it there. That'll free up hard drive space for you. Not to mention, if your computer crashes, you won't lose everything. Your laptop was like a walking time bomb."

I raise my eyebrows. "I thought I was saving it to the server."

"No, old man, just because you named the folder server doesn't mean it was actually being saved there."

"Smartass," I grunt, but then soften my gaze. "Thank you."

He nods. "No problem. It'd been a bitch to get that stuff back if your hard drive failed. I could do it, but it'd still be a bitch."

"Last year, my laptop crashed and we couldn't recover anything," I grumble. "Our IT department basically told me to get over it because there wasn't anything I could do."

His grin is smug. "Because they're incompetent. I could have done it."

"You're arrogant," I huff.

"You like it."

I do. I love that he's brilliant and haughty about it. It's nice seeing him confident about something besides the bedroom, since this past week, he's been struggling to stay afloat.

"Any cases you need help with? I may not be great

with computers, but I'm pretty fucking good at every-thing else," I toss back at him.

He laughs but then his face grows stony. "I want to see about getting Malachi and Xavier moved."

"Who?"

"The Bryant kids. Enzo said—"

I put up a hand to stop him. "Slow down. I thought your case was against their last foster home. They've been moved already, right?"

His brows furl. "They have, but I don't like it. Enzo said he didn't like the vibe either. Something about the new foster home feels fucking fishy."

"I didn't realize you and Lorenzo Tauber were so close."

"We've just talked a few times about the case and the boys." His eyes drift outside, and this young man suddenly seems older than his twenty-five years. "They've just been through so much."

"Yeah, kids in the system often have it especially hard." I nudge his bare foot under the table with the toe of my boot. "But kids out of the system don't al-ways have it easy either."

He returns his attention on me. "Some kids, though, like Mel, have something good. I just want that for these kids. No one deserves to feel unsafe in their own home." His jaw clenches and his brown eyes flare. My stare has fallen on his slightly swollen lip that still bears a split from his father last night.

"Enzo's their caseworker. Is the new home not fit?"

His brows knit harder together. "That's the thing. It is. Everything from the outside looks fine. It's just... he says the way the foster parents look at the children feels threatening."

I let out a sigh and massage the tension forming at the base of my skull. "We can't pull kids from homes based on feelings. You know how things work, Nick. We need more than that. Get us more and we can have a judge intervene. Until then, we can't do anything."

He grinds his teeth together and rises from the table before grabbing his plate up and stalking over to the sink. I follow after him and hug him from behind. His muscles are taught and coiled for a fight, but the moment I embrace him, he relaxes.

"It's unfair," he murmurs. "It's so unfair."

I kiss his shoulder. "Get me more and we'll make it happen. I'm not saying we give up on them, I'm just saying we'll have to work harder."

His plate clatters into the sink and then he twists

around to face me. Intensity burns in his stare as he crashes his lips to mine. He backs me against the fridge and kisses me hard. When he finally pulls his mouth from mine, his hot breath tickling my lips, he smiles.

"Thank you. Thank you for helping me."

I don't think we're simply talking about the kids.

We're talking about so much more.

"Always, babe," I rasp out. And I fucking mean it too.

ELEVEN

Nick

"I'd help you finish but I have to be in court in thirty minutes. I'll see you at the office later," Dane says, as he scrapes the passenger side window of my car free of snow. "Don't forget tonight we're going out with Max."

Max.

Just the way he says his name with a slight happy lilt of his voice grates on my nerves. I'm not a fan of Max. The good, fair judge or not...he hit his best friend because he put a move on him. Every time I think of that, my blood boils.

"See ya," I grunt out.

He slaps my ass with his gloved hand on the way back to his car and I can't help but smile. Yesterday was reminiscent of the weekend we met. Just the two of us. Locked away alone, free to spend uninterrupted time together. We watched movies, ate, and fucked. The last one more so than the first two. Even now, just thinking of being inside his tight ass has my dick twitching in my slacks.

Thank God it's cold as fuck because my erection leaves as quickly as it arrives. I finish clearing my car of the lingering snow and head to the office. The nearer I get, the more my nerves begin to fray. Soon, no matter how hard I try, I'll be forced to see my dad.

As soon as I'm in the building, I make a beeline for my office. I attempt to close the door behind me but Susan follows me inside. Her lips are painted bright pink today and her boobs are threatening to spill from her top. The way she bites on her bottom lip and leans across the desk to hand me a file tells me she wants them to.

She briefs me on my missed phone calls and upcoming appointments, all the while jiggling her tits at me. I'm about to open my mouth and blurt out that I fuck boys, not girls, when a knock resounds behind her on the open door.

"Oh, Mr. Stratton," she coos as she stands upright and sashays over to him.

My father's eyes drop to her tits and he grins

wickedly at her. "Yes, Susan?"

"Good morning."

"It's a wonderful morning," he agrees as he eye-fucks her. "Can you be a dear and run along to Starbucks for me? We're out of the good coffee, and I can't drink the backup shit in the breakroom."

She shifts on her heels and then glances outside where the snow still covers the sidewalks. "Uh, sure."

Before she gets past him, he leans in and whispers something to her before giving her a soft pat to her ass that has her giggling. Then, she scurries off, leaving me with this motherfucker. As soon as she's gone, he closes the door. His dark brown gaze clashes with mine, fury blazing in them.

"Your mother has been worried," he says blandly, despite the fire in his eyes.

I lean back in my chair, threading my fingers together and letting them rest in my lap. "She didn't call."

He narrows his eyes at me. "Where were you?"

"A friend's," I lie.

"Which friend? Waylon?"

I don't remind him Waylon was an ex-boyfriend, not a friend. Instead, I shake my head. "Nope. New friend."

He sits on the corner of my desk and picks up a heavy, glass paperweight. His eyes are on me as he rolls it around in his hand. I'm tense and ready to duck in case he decides he wants to throw that shit at me. I wouldn't put it past him.

"Does your new friend work here?" he challenges, tossing the paperweight up in the air and catching it. To an outsider, this would all seem casual. To an insider, I know my dad is about three seconds from losing his shit.

"I'm not jeopardizing our jobs," I say coolly. Never mind the fact that technically I am. Probably, to any other employer, it'd be a big fucking deal. But we're talking about Dane here. He doesn't seem the type to go on a firing spree when I get bored and leave him high and dry.

My gut hollows out.

The past couple of nights at his house have been refreshing. Relaxing and right. I don't know what I've been looking for, but this sure feels close to it, whatever it is.

"Good," he says, setting the paperweight down. "Keep it that way. I'm watching, son."

My phone buzzes and I expect it to be Dane done with court. Instead, it's Enzo calling through.

"Hello?"

"Something's not right," he growls down the line.

I sit up straight. "The boys?"

"Not just the boys. Cora and Jenna too. I did some digging and this couple is friends with Juanita Aikens."

I've been fixated on the boys because they're my case and I've seen the reports of the physical abuse from their parents as well, but the girls were placed in the same home. Are there no safe places for these kids?

"What do we do?" I demand, frustration souring the coffee in my stomach.

"I was hoping you'd know."

We're both silent as we think. Enzo is older than me, in his late thirties. He's been a social worker since he graduated from college, according to our conversations. It's his passion. Unfortunately, aside from this specific case, being an attorney is not *my* passion.

"Let me talk to August and see what we can do," I tell him before hanging up.

I rise from my chair, snag the file, and stalk from my office. When I get to August's, I hear him laugh. I didn't know he even knew how. As soon as I step in his doorway, his features turn to ice once more. The girl standing near him has candy-apple red hair—something unnatural and straight from a bottle. She gives his shoulder a squeeze, murmurs a goodbye, and then slips past me.

"Sorry to interrupt," I tell him gruffly. "It's important."

He waves my words off. "Don't worry about it. What's going on? The Bryant case?"

I nod as I plop down in the chair across from his desk. "Enzo is worried they've gotten out of one bad situation to land in another one."

"There was no home study?" he asks.

Flipping open the file, I find a copy of the newest home study for their current foster situation and point at it. "Perfect."

He pulls it closer and skims over it, his face impassive. "It's bullshit. Too perfect." His sigh is heavy. "Not all foster homes are abusive."

"I know, but these poor kids have shitty luck. I can smell a rat from a mile away. So can Enzo. And you…" I trail off and gesture to the file. "You smell it too. How do we intervene? Everything so far is by the books. Everything I learned in law school. What happens when it's not by the books?"

August frowns. "I can get a judge to issue an emergency well-check per an anonymous tip. Then, we'll send in CPS. Enzo can do his job—what we can't do. We'll present our findings to the judge and go from there. That's all we can do for now."

"How will you get him to grant it for you if you don't actually have an anonymous tip?" I ask in confusion.

"We have our 'anonymous' tip. The judge doesn't need to know it was Enzo." He grins wickedly. "Now get out of here and research some good foster homes. Let's make sure they get sent someplace safe next time. I'll handle the rest."

As I rise, he starts tapping on his computer and then immediately curses.

"I fucking hate this thing," he grumbles.

I walk over and see he, like Dane, has eight million programs running all at once. "Save everything and close it. Then, restart. When was the last time you rebooted this thing?"

He grumbles. "I close the damn thing every evening when I leave the office."

"You put it in sleep mode with multiple programs continuing to run. It's never able to refresh. Imagine starting your day with the leftover coffee in your mug from the day before," I tell him, shrugging.

His lip curls up. "You've made your point."

I smirk and give him a wave. "Don't forget to tell me I'm right later."

"Yeah, yeah…"

I spend the better part of the day on the phone with August and Enzo, off and on. August made good on his abilities to get the judge to sign off on what we needed. Enzo wasted no time and has been at the home ever since. He's been doing the home check and later, he'll be interviewing the children living there, including the Bryant boys. Whatever he finds, we'll present to the judge in a couple of days.

When I see Dane storm through the office with his phone glued to his ear, I can't help but follow after him to tell him the good news. He's griping to someone and after eavesdropping a bit, I can tell it's Janice.

"She's fine," he grumbles. "If something were wrong, we'd be the first to know about it."

I can hear her yapping on the other line. His eyes meet mine and the hard, irritated glare dissolves as a smile tugs at his lips. Standing beside his desk in his long black dress coat, and looking dapper as fuck with his suit underneath, my mouth waters for a taste of him. His eyes darken at my look and he motions with his head at the door. I push it closed and lock it behind me. She continues to talk to him and he just grunts out words of agreement as I prowl his way. When I grip his dick through his slacks, I'm happy to find he's hard and just as horny as I am.

When I drop to one knee and begin working at his belt, his palm cradles the side of my head. Such a tender touch despite the fact he's about to get his dick sucked in his office. This should be filthy and wrong and fucking taboo since he's my boss, but the way he touches me erases all of that. It confuses me for a moment. But then his thick cock is punching against his black boxers, begging for its own touch. I free his length and admire the angry crown of his cock. Red— nearly purple—his pre-cum glistening from the slit at the top, eager to be licked. His dark hair is cropped short, making his dick seem longer and every bit as distinguished as he is. Who the fuck has a gentleman- ly dick? Dane, that's who.

He says some things to her and I decide I want to distract him from that awful woman. Jealousy over the woman he once cared deeply for and loved has me running my tongue over the tip of his dick in a teasing way sure to make him crazy. His soft touch fades as he fists my hair, messing up the gel. I look up and revel in the way his gray eyes blaze with intensity as he peers down at me. From my vantage point, he's a god. Tall, powerful, radiating delicious energy. I'm on my knees, worshipping this god. Begging for a taste.

Usually, I like being the one in his position. But with Dane, it's nice to reverse the roles a bit. He looks hot as fuck in his three-piece suit and coat. His tie is one I'd love to wrap around his wrists and bind him with later. Until that time, I work the base of his cock with my fist as I suck on the top half.

"I've gotta go," he grunts out. "Congrats to you too."

He hangs up and tosses the phone on his desk. His full attention is now on me.

"Fuck, you're so good at this." I love the way his voice sounds husky and raw and unsure.

I slip my hand away so I can take him deeper into my throat. He groans, his grip on my hair tightening as he begins to lose control. His hips thrust into me, causing his giant dick to ravage my throat. Fuck, he's the biggest I've ever had and the thought thrills me. My throat is being rubbed raw by his massive cock and I love every second of it. Later, at the bar, I'll numb it with some tequila. Until then, I enjoy the burn.

"Yessss…" he hisses and his body trembles. "Fuck, Nick, you're killing me."

I swallow and a hum vibrates through me. It's enough to send him over the edge. A feral roar that he doesn't do well to keep contained rips from him. His heat—explosive and furious—bursts down my throat. I drink his pleasure down, satisfied that I can bring this once "straight" man to absolute bliss. Once he's done and I've swallowed every salty drop, he pulls away, his dick slipping past my lips. My saliva tethers us together for a moment before it breaks free.

"I like the way you taste," I tell him with a devious smile.

His cock that had started to soften twitches. I love that he's always turned on for me. He's admitted to me that he thought his sex life was dwindling. And it had been…with Janice. But with someone new and exciting, it's like his beast has been awakened. I woke that beast.

He stuffs his wet cock back into his slacks as I stand. Once he's decent, he steps closer and grips my hips. His mouth is on mine the next instant. Desperate and hungry. We kiss wildly until we're both breathing heavily and groaning for more.

"I have half a mind to cancel tonight's plans and just take you home so we continue this," he rasps out, his lips peppering kisses all over my mouth. He nips at my sore bottom lip.

I'm about to open my mouth to agree with him when someone knocks on his door. We break apart and panic flashes in his gray eyes. I give him a reassuring smile as I go to answer the door. It falls away when I find myself staring at my father.

He glowers at me. Glances at Dane and then back at me. The vein in his neck bulges and his skin turns nearly purple.

"I need to speak with you, son," he snarls.

I can feel Dane's stare boring into me as I leave without so much as a backward glance. I follow Dad to my office, and I'm barely in the door before he slams it shut and has me shoved against the wall.

"Who the hell do you think you are?" he bellows, unable to keep his tone down despite the fact Susan can probably hear every word.

"I don't know what you're talking about," I snap.

"You're a useless whore like your mother. You

fuck whatever benefits you at the time," he sneers. "If this shit blows up in your face, it affects my job too. This is one of the best firms. I need this partnership and these connections if I want to run for office."

Always about him.

Fuck the fact that for the first time in my life, I'm happy. There's something with Dane that I actually want for myself. It's not fleeting either. I can feel it taking root inside me. If I take the time to nourish it, it could turn into something lasting. Something real.

"Are we done?" I snap. "I feel done."

With lightning speed, he backhands me. My hands fist, eager to punch him in the face, but I refrain. I glare at him with all the hate I can muster.

"We're done," I growl. "Get the hell out of my office."

He steps back and grabs the paperweight. His arm rears back but before he throws it, the door softly clicks open. Dane steps inside and kicks it shut behind him. He stalks over to my dad and forcefully takes the paperweight from his hand. Dad has the sense to look shamed, and he cowers under Dane's formidable strength and intimidation.

"Touch my employee again and I'll sue you fucking dry," Dane hisses. "I'll ruin you for this."

Dad gapes at him in shock before his features twist into a hateful scowl that he shoots my way. But his words are for Dane. "You think fucking my boy is something special, man? He fucks anything with a dick. Now, he's just fucking you to fuck with me." Dad's nostrils flare as though he truly believes his words.

"Chandler," Dane starts, his words cool and even, "you're going to leave this office and go back to yours. If I see you step out of line again, you're out of here. I don't care what the hell you think it is your son is doing, you leave that for me to worry about. This is my firm, not yours. You have a temporary partnership and it'd do you good to remember that."

Dad glowers at us both, his jaw clenching with words he desperately seems to want to say.

Dane sets the paperweight down on the desk and then grabs Dad's tie, wrapping it around his fist. He pulls Dad close to his face. "And man to man," he bites out. "If you lay one goddamned finger on my boyfriend again, I'll knock every one of your teeth out."

Dad's eyes widen in shock at Dane's words. Hell, I'm shocked too. Not only did he defend me from my dad's abuse, but he just fucking claimed me.

"Go," Dane orders, releasing my father.

"Remember what I've told you."

Dad gives him a clipped nod and storms from the office, slamming the door behind him on his way out. As soon as he's gone, Dane strides over to me and cups my jaw with his strong hand as he surveys the damage.

"What an asshole," he seethes, anger still flaring in his gray eyes. The storm is waging within them.

"Yeah."

He kisses my sore lip softly. "I'm sorry."

I smile. "Don't be sorry. Things are looking up."

His mouth slants over mine and I part my lips, eager for another taste of him. I don't get why I'm so addicted to everything about him. It's starting to make me lose my mind. Our tongues slide against each other. Hot, slippery, wet. We kiss until we're both panting and our hard dicks are an annoying problem that can't easily be solved in my office.

"A couple of drinks to celebrate. Janice was congratulating me on the finalization of our divorce," he says, his voice hoarse, "So, we'll have a toast and then I want you naked in my bed."

I grin at him. "Two drinks, and then I'm tying you to the headboard. I need to reward you for that little show."

The playfulness in his stare fades as he leans his forehead against mine. "It wasn't a show, Nick. It was real. All of this is real. And I'll be damned if I let some pompous prick touch one hair of what's mine."

Mine?

The possessive way with which he says the words has me relaxing against him. This time, we kiss softly. Unspoken promises are told in a simple kiss. My lips and tongue say what I can't seem to articulate.

You're mine too, Dane.

And fuck if that doesn't scare the hell out of me.

TWELVE

Dane

Ever since Nick and I hooked up at the hotel, I've been dying to tell Max about this new revelation. That I'm finally doing what I want. Seeing a guy who turns my world upside and that I've never been happier. But then I remember the night from college so clearly. The night I nearly lost my best friend. As we walk in the bar to meet him and his sons-in-law, my stomach is in knots. If it's anything like that night I let my secret slip, things might go badly.

When I see Max wave from a high-top table, I give him a nod and then look over my shoulder at Nick. He's scowling and it reminds me so much of August that I let out a chuckle. I make my way over to the table and Max stands to shake my hand, before pulling me in for a hug. At one time, I was truly in love with my best friend and I wasn't much younger than Nick when my he tore my heart from my chest. It took months and months to repair what I'd nearly broken.

Now, I'm glad we didn't fuck around. I wouldn't have Mel. He wouldn't have the girls. We'd have lived different lives. Probably would have fucked up our friendship in the end. Max is remarried now and happy as hell with Dorian. I'm embarking on something extremely gratifying with Nick. It was better this way.

"Max," I greet as we pull away. "This is Nick." I bite my tongue, suddenly hesitant to explain just who Nick is to me. "We work together at the firm."

Max nods and offers his hand. "Nick."

Nick shakes it but he only manages a nod. Max, always nice and friendly, releases his hand but doesn't take offense. He introduces his sons-in-law.

"This is Miles, my oldest daughter Olivia's husband," Max says. "And that shifty-eyed asshole over there is Drew. He's married to my youngest daughter, Soph."

"Nick Stratton," Nick says, nodding to both men.

Miles arches a brow and smirks. He's a suit-wearing prick like the rest of us but the difference is, Miles looks like he's a damn lumberjack. Wild, dark hair that he barely tames on top of his head. But it's the beard that says it all. Drew, on the other hand, is the preppy bastard. Khakis and polos are his usual outfits. He's a physical therapist and dresses like a boring bastard, but he's hot. Both men are attractive as hell. When I'd been introduced long ago, I'd been unable to keep from checking them out. I shoot Nick a questioning look to see if he finds them good looking too, but his gaze is hard and guarded. I'm not sure what the hell is up with him.

I settle on a barstool beside Max and Nick sits next to me. Miles launches into a story about his club. He owns a sex club downtown. If Nick is surprised by this, he makes no indication. Every time Max laughs or says something, though, he tenses or fists his hand.

Maybe he's pissed I didn't introduce him as my lover or boyfriend or whatever the hell we are. But I don't know what the protocol is for this stuff.

We spend the next hour shooting the shit. Nick chats easily with Miles and Drew, but ignores Max to the best of his ability. Later, I'm going to ask him what his deal is.

"I'm going to take a piss," Max says before sauntering off.

Nick slides off his stool and stalks after him.

"Guess he had to piss too," Miles says, shrugging.

Drew snorts. "He's going to kick his ass."

I nearly choke on my beer. "What?"

Drew's brow lifts. "Have you not seen the way your boyfriend has been shooting him death glares all night?"

"He's your boyfriend?" Miles asks. "I mean, I knew you two were fucking, but—"

"How did you know we're fucking?" I demand.

Miles laughs. "How close you two sit together. The way you look at each other. My son's gay, in case you forgot. I've been around two guys in love long enough to know what it looks like."

"We're not in lov—"

"But he is your boyfriend, right?" Drew asks, smirking. "This doesn't seem like a one-night stand. Not with how possessive he is over you. I mean, he's about to punch your best friend in the teeth."

"Fuck," I grunt, hopping off my stool and tearing off toward the bathroom. Miles and Drew bellow with laughter behind me. Fucking assholes.

I storm down the hallway and push into the bathroom. Sure enough, Nick is in Max's face and Max is glowering at him. Both men are seconds from tearing each other's heads off.

"Whoa. What the hell did I miss back there?" I demand.

Nick turns his head my way and his nostrils flare with fury. "Your sexuality isn't some joke or some injustice toward the good fucking judge. It's you. It's who you are. And because of him, you were forced to live twenty something years with that bitch."

"You should pick better friends," Max snaps my way. "This guy is a real winner."

I step between them and push Nick away gently.

"Calm down," I tell him. "You can't go around shoving people when they piss you off."

Max grunts in agreement which sets Nick off again.

"And you can't fucking hit people because they're gay!" Nick roars at him.

"It was a drunk attempt at a kiss, that never should have happened, decades ago," Max growls. "How this is any of your business, kid, is beyond me. I don't know why you told him this shit anyway, Dane. I never told anyone."

I turn to regard Max. "I thought it was more…"

His jaw clenches. "It wasn't more. I was clear about that."

"Because you fucking punched him," Nick seethes.

Max glares at him until his mind seems to figure out a puzzle and the anger melts away. His green eyes dart my way. "But you've been dating women after Janice."

"I have," I agree.

His shoulders relax. "So, what the hell is all this about?"

I turn and look at Nick. Beautiful, strong Nick. His neck muscles are ticking and his jaw clenches as he stares down my best friend. I hold my hand out. Nick's brown eyes fall to my hand and he takes it. Shrugging, I turn to face Max, who stares at me in shock.

"I'm with Nick now."

He blinks at me. "What?"

I tug Nick closer to me. Nick hangs an arm over my shoulders as if to confirm my words. "I'm his boyfriend," Nick tells him, his tone smug.

Mr. I Don't Do Relationships loves that he can throw this in Max's face. It makes my chest squeeze that he's so adamant about standing up for me about something that happened forever ago, and then staking his claim over me.

Max frowns at me. "I..." He looks sorry. Like he wants to say it. But he's still clearly riled by Nick. "I need a drink." With that, he storms from the bathroom.

Nick slides his arm away and grips my ass. "He needed to know."

I turn and grip his jaw so I can admire his handsome face. "That I'm gay?"

"That we're together," he tells me. "That one homophobic moment in his life sent you in a direction you never wanted to be. He needed to know. That you had to wait this long to finally be fucking happy. As your best friend, he needed to know he set that in motion."

"I'm a grown man, Nick. My life turned out the way it did because I made certain choices. Max and I had one bad moment for a lifetime of friendship. People make mistakes. I should have never tried to kiss him. But he's not responsible for my hesitancy to try to be with a man. That's all on me." I kiss him on his pouty lips. "It took you to give me the confidence to try."

He smiles and I want to taste it on my tongue. I kiss him deeper. Eventually, he pulls away to stare intently at me. "We're doing more than just trying and we're doing it together."

I lift a brow in amusement. "And you're my boy-friend now?"

"I'm sure as fuck not your boy toy," he retorts, a devilish glint in his eyes.

"Hmm," I tease. "When you were on your knees earlier in my office, I wasn't sure."

He nips at my bottom lip as he grips my dick through my slacks. "I'll remind you who's in charge later when I have my dick down your throat and your helpless ass is tied to your bed."

His wicked smile undoes me.

"Buy me a drink, boss," I say with a wink.

He smirks. "Now we're talking."

"Knock, knock."

Nick looks up from his paperwork, stressed and tired, but manages a smile for me. "Hey."

"Merry Christmas." I toss him a package. "And before you panic, everyone in the office gets one."

He relaxes in his chair as he opens the box. Everyone gets five-hundred-dollar Visa check cards on Christmas Eve each year. Nick's not the only one who likes playing Santa.

"What's your schedule like? Can we cut out of here early?" he asks, a hint of excitement in his voice.

It's Christmas Eve. I don't have any clients, and we usually close up around three anyway. We can cut out at noon instead.

"Yeah, let's get out of here. Eager to shop?" I ask as he stands to collect his coat.

"I know just the place. I need to make a phone call first. Grab your stuff and let's go," he orders, grinning.

His joyful attitude is catching and I hurry to my office to grab my things. August's office is dark. I'm not sure he even made it in today. Chandler is nowhere to be seen. The place is half dead with all the lawyers bailing. I slap Susan's desk as I round the corner.

"Tell everyone they can go home early. Lock it up and get out of here," I instruct.

She squeals and starts tapping out an email to everyone. "Merry Christmas, boss!"

I chuckle all the way to my office. My phone has a few texts from Mel, reminding me about tomorrow. As if I'd forget Christmas with my baby girl. I reply back that we'll be there and that I love her. After I pull on my coat and grab my bag, I find Nick looking hot as hell, standing in the doorway as he rapid-fire texts with someone.

"Should I be jealous?" I tease.

He flashes me an evil grin. "Maybe. The idea of you jealous is actually a turn on."

I laugh and swat at him on my way out the door. "I don't need to get jealous to turn you on. You're pretty easy, babe."

His snort earns a few glances our way as we walk toward the elevators. "Easy, huh?"

"I had my dick in your mouth within hours of meeting you," I remind him, loving the way his brown eyes flare with the reminder.

We step inside the elevator and the doors close behind us. I shove him into the corner with my body and then attack his lips. Our kiss is feverish and wild until the elevator dings. Then, the doors open and we pull away. It isn't until we're in my Porsche and driving that I finally ask where we're going.

"We have to make a pit stop by the house to change. Then, it's off to Target. I have a whole list of presents I have to buy and wrap before four." His smile is contagious.

"Four, huh? Cutting it a little close, don't you think? Most people don't wait until the very last minute on Christmas Eve to start their shopping."

He turns my way and grips my thigh. "That was Enzo."

I think of Lorenzo Tauber with his mess of dark, curly hair, perpetual five o'clock shadow, and always hooded hazel eyes. Enzo, someone I've dealt with over the years with many of my cases involving children, is someone to definitely be jealous of.

Nick squeezes my thigh and chuckles. "We weren't making a date. Well, actually, we were. He's set something up with the foster parents to bring the kids some presents."

I glance over at Nick and he's buzzing with excitement. I've never seen him so…eager. Like a little kid on Christmas Eve, waiting to sit in Santa's lap. But in his story, he's the Santa and he's trying to save Christmas. My chest aches as I realize Nick makes me feel something deep inside me that's never existed before. Something strong. Something that grows by the day. Something that will ultimately consume the both of us if we'll let it.

I'm ready.

I thread my fingers with his. "Let's do this."

"Let's do this," he agrees.

I'm talking about so much more than tonight.

I'm talking about forever.

THIRTEEN

Nick

The list Enzo sent me was helpful except when it came to the two girls. Sure, I have a sister but I didn't know where half the shit they wanted was at Target. Luckily, Dane has a daughter and handled that easily. I was in charge of the boys and could have spent a lot more than my gift card on them. When I got to the toy aisle, I thought about everything they don't have and wanted to buy them the whole store. Dane was gentle but firm when he reminded me we were going off a specific list from their caseworker and needed to stick with it.

Now that we're on the way to the foster home, I'm nervous. My palms are sweaty and my Santa beard itches my cheeks. I'd worn it into Target and got a couple of squeals from kids doing last-minute shopping with their parents.

"It's snowing," Dane says, grinning my way.

"The kids will love that."

As we drive, Dane reaches over and rests his palm on my thigh. I'd been jittery and my leg was jumping but with his comforting strength warming my thigh, I relax some.

"Nick, I need you to listen," he rumbles. "No matter what we see there, it's not our place to intervene. There are laws and as attorneys, we follow them. We've been granted a visit by the foster parents, and we'd do best to be respectful while in their home. It's what's best for everyone."

I let out a heavy sigh. "What if they're assholes?"

"We let the judge determine whether or not the kids are fit to stay there. All we can do is our part. You're doing more than your part. It's admirable. However, you can't let it consume you. I'm sure it'll be sad, but don't do anything that you'll regret later or will impact the kids." He pats my leg. "With that suit comes great responsibility." His playful words at the end have me relaxing again.

"This is why I suck at being a lawyer," I grumble. "I don't like sitting back and waiting for the law to play out in favor of the victims. I want to step in and bring justice for them."

He turns down a dark street and his eyes dart toward me. "In a perfect world, that's what we do. But in this imperfect, complicated one, we do the best we can with what we can."

I can't help but chuckle. "Growing up with my dad and hearing the constant jabs about attorneys being awful and wicked, I must say, it's a stereotype. Not all attorneys are like my dad. Some of us care."

We pull into a driveway behind a black sedan. Once we step out of the car, another man gets out. He walks over to Dane and shakes his hand. When I make my way to him, he smiles.

"You must be Nick. Pleased to finally meet you."

"Nick," Dane says. "Meet Lorenzo Tauber. Enzo, this is St. Nick."

We all chuckle but then I grow serious when I look over at the house.

"And they're expecting us?" I ask, nerves clenching in my stomach.

"They're expecting a visit from Santa and some gifts. The foster mom wasn't keen on a visit from the caseworker two days this week, but I convinced her this was something we do often and not part of the home study," Enzo says. "We need to tread lightly."

His hand clasps my shoulder and his brows deepen into a frown. "It's easy to get angry when we see injustices done to these kids. But for us to protect them and help them, we have to remain cool. I'm trusting you by taking you here with me."

I nod and Dane gives me a smug grin. I've received the same lecture twice now. Do I look like the type of guy who's going to waltz in there and come out with a kid in each arm?

Dane pops open the hatch and pulls out the giant red sack filled with wrapped presents for the children on Enzo's list. I adjust my beard and pull on my cap that comes with fake white, curly hair. I'm a thin Santa but hopefully the kids won't mind. The ones at Target surely didn't.

Enzo walks ahead of us. The snow dusts his black coat and he slips a little going up the steps. Dane and I are more careful going up. By the time we reach the porch, Enzo has rung the doorbell.

A woman answers the door and eyes us all suspiciously before waving us inside.

"Mrs. Friedman, thank you for allowing us to come," Enzo says politely, his voice a cold pitch I've never heard from him in all the phone conversations we've had.

She nods. "Not like I had a choice." Her eyes narrow at Dane and I, but she doesn't say much more on the matter. Once inside, I take note that the house isn't as warm as Dane keeps his. I'm already tallying everything at fault here. Like the lingering scent of cigarette smoke. The fact that there isn't one single Christmas decoration. That the kids aren't in the living room and the home is creepily quiet.

I shoot Dane a glare and he shakes his head slightly at me as if to tell me to calm down. But I can't calm down. The coldness of this home reminds me so much of my own. Such a stark contrast of Dane's house. At his house, you can fucking relax, and it's warm. Even Dane has a Christmas tree up with presents beneath.

"Kids! Get down here now!" Mrs. Friedman yells up the stairs.

Enzo's jaw clenches but his features remain impassive. Dane's brows have now furled together. I'm tense as well but I know my part. I'm Santa. For just a short while, my job is to make these kids happy. This, I can do.

I find the recliner and take a seat. Dane sets the bag beside me and leans against the wall, as though he wants to blend into it and observe. Enzo is our liaison here and smiles at me before winking. This is good. We're doing okay.

A girl comes down the stairs holding a toddler on her hip. Her dark brown hair is smoothed straight except for the part the smaller girl is twisting around on her fingers. She glances over at us with hard green eyes and my stomach hollows out. This girl has seen some things, if the untrusting stare she pins on every adult in the room is any indication.

"Jenna," Enzo greets, his voice rough. "Hi there, Cora." His voice softens as he greets the little blonde girl. Cora buries her face in Jenna's neck as if to hide from him. His shoulders hunch as though he's dejected.

"Boys!" Mrs. Friedman bellows. "Get down here now! We have company!"

I flinch at her yelling. Both girls do the same and it has Enzo stepping toward them in a protective manner. Finally, three boys, including the Bryant brothers, start clomping down the steps. One boy has fire-engine red hair and looks to be about four. Malachi, at only seven, seems to be the protector over them just as Jenna looks after Cora. His arm is slung over his younger brother Xavier's shoulders. Malachi and Xavier both have the palest gray eyes that are a stark contrast to their dark brown skin.

"Joseph," Mrs. Friedman barks to the red-haired boy. "Santa is here. Isn't that what you've been begging for all week?"

He peers up and his green eyes light up upon seeing me. I smile at him.

"Ho! Ho! Ho!" I say in my jolliest voice.

All the tension and fear that had him in its clutches is gone as he bolts my way. He climbs into my lap and tugs at my beard.

"You're here!"

"Of course I am," I tell him. "Have you been a good boy this year?"

His smile falls and he looks over at Mrs. Friedman for the answer. She simply purses his lips together.

"No," he whispers, fat tears welling in his eyes.

I grit my teeth, swallowing the urge to tell the mean-ass lady to get lost. "I don't believe that," I tell him. "In fact, you're on my good list, Joseph."

He swipes away the tears and gives me a hopeful look. "I am?"

Nodding, I motion at Dane to hand me the gifts for Joseph. The boy oohs and ahhs over the wrapped gifts. As he opens his dump truck, pajamas, blocks, and stuffed animal, he shrieks with glee. Four presents were all I was allowed to buy for each of these kids. Growing up, had I only received four presents, I would have been devastated. This boy seems like this might very well be the best Christmas ever.

"Thank you, Santa," he says happily and hugs my neck.

I hug him back and catch the stare of the youngest Bryant brother. Xavier watches me sadly. My heart cracks open right then.

"That's enough, Joseph," Mrs. Friedman snaps. "Jenna, take Cora over there."

Jenna glowers at Mrs. Friedman but obeys. I catch Enzo staring after them with a look of heartbreak that must match my own. How can he handle a job like this? Every day would be torture.

Cora starts squealing when Jenna tries to sit her in my lap. She's scared. Poor thing.

"Do you want to sit with her?" I ask Jenna.

Jenna frowns as though she doesn't want to, but is thinking about Cora. "I'm a little too big."

"I'm strong," I assure her with a wink.

I earn a small smile from Jenna and she sits down on my knee. Cora, a little curious now that Jenna is sitting too, turns to regard me with big, watery blue eyes. She reaches out and touches my nose.

"Santa?" she whispers, so softly I almost didn't hear.

"Merry Christmas, Cora. You've been a good girl this year. I brought you some presents," I tell her.

"Sissy too?" she asks.

I know they're not sisters, but it's adorable that Cora seems to think they are. "Sissy too," I agree. "Both the best girls on my list."

Cora grins a toothy smile at me.

Dane hands me their gifts one by one. Cora is happy with her soft, crushed red velvet nightgown with a picture of Rudolph on the front. She loves the doll and coloring book, but it's the stuffed koala bear that she seems to love the most.

Jenna is able to ease her to the floor where she can play with her new things. I hand Jenna her first gift. She's so much like Christina that it hurts. They're both pretty in that "young woman with determination glinting in their eyes" kind of way, but there is an innocence hiding in Jenna that doesn't exist in my sister. Something that should be protected. Fuck, this is hard seeing these kids. I want to help them all. I want to pull them from this house and put them someplace where they'll be happy.

"These are soft," Jenna murmurs as she pets the

flannel pajama set. "And warm." Tears glisten in her green eyes and one snakes down her cheek. From across the room, I catch Enzo's stare. He's tense and coiled, and his hands are fisted at his sides. *I know the feeling, buddy.*

She opens the next present. It's a pretty journal with a pen attached. A smile tugs at her lips. Then, she opens the bag with a necklace with angel wings on it, and finally, a kindle. Her mouth opens and she lets out a gasp.

"I can't afford any books, though," she whispers softly, enough for only us to hear.

But Dane leans down and grins. "Santa's helper loaded a gift card on there while Santa was busy wrapping the other presents."

She regards him with a huge smile. "Thank you."

Jenna helps Cora and together, they move their things to the end of the couch near where Enzo is standing. Mrs. Friedman gets distracted by yelling at Joseph. My eyes are still on Enzo and the girls, so I witness something I wasn't meant to see. He discreetly hands her a phone. She pockets it in her hoodie pocket and they continue on as if nothing ever happened.

A lifeline.

He just gave her a way to reach him if she needs help.

I'd run over and hug him if I didn't have the Bryant boys edging closer to me. Malachi tries to get his younger brother to sit down first, but the little boy isn't having it. With a heavy, too old for his years, sigh, Malachi sits on my lap.

"You, too, were a good boy," I tell him.

He frowns and shrugs. "I guess."

"You are," I tell him firmly. "You are strong and resilient."

His icy gray eyes lift to mine. The strength in him wavers as his eyes tear up. "I'm not strong."

"You are."

He smiles. "I am."

Dane squeezes my shoulder briefly as he hands me Malachi's first gift. He appreciates the pajamas and then laughs over his Rubik's cube. His eyes light up when he opens the Lego set and he grins again when he unwraps a Darth Vader action figure. The boy who seemed too old for his age moments ago is now every bit the seven-year-old he's supposed to be. I wish I could pause the moment and let him be a kid a little while longer.

Finally, after some coaxing, I get Xavier into my

lap. For someone hesitant, he warms up quickly. I get hugged from the young boy and he doesn't let go.

"I don't want toys for Christmas, Santa." His voice is croaky like a frog. So cute.

"You don't?" I ask, surprised, shooting Enzo a panicked look.

He's too busy pretending to make Cora's koala talk. She giggles and the sound brings life to the sad home.

"No," Xavier croaks. He leans in and whispers in my ear, "I don't want anyone to hurt my big brother and me."

I hug him to me for a long moment, blinking away the tears from my eyes. Dane, having overheard, peers down at him with such a heartbreaking stare. As though, if he knew how, he'd make this little boy's dreams come true.

"I'm Santa," I tell him, patting his back. "I have my ways of making miracles happen. Can you hang in there and look after your brother until I talk to my elves?"

He nods with such a hopeful look, I feel as though my heart is trying to claw its way out of my chest to hug him. With the sweet appreciation that the other children had, Xavier opens his gifts too. Matching pajamas with his brother. A puppy puzzle and an Iron Man action figure. But his favorite is the stuffed penguin to which he hugs, and then burrows against my chest, like he'd like to stay there for a while. I wish I could keep him there.

"I'm hungry," Joseph whimpers.

Mrs. Friedman narrows her eyes at him. "No snacks after supper."

I start to open my mouth but Enzo shakes his head. Fuck, this is hard.

"It's time for Santa to go," Mrs. Friedman says coolly. "He has other children to see."

Xavier clings to me as though he doesn't want me to go. I don't want to fucking go either. Mrs. Friedman walks over and plucks him from my lap, making him yelp. I rise quickly to my feet, towering over her. She isn't fazed by my size and simply walks over to the front door to open it.

"Thank you for allowing us to come," Enzo says in a false, cheery tone. He shoots one last look at Jenna and Cora before walking out the door. Dane follows but I linger, letting my stare bounce from kid to kid before landing on the Bryant boys.

They both watch me with sad gray eyes but their shoulders are squared. They're trying to be brave. To be strong. I clench my fists. Two arms, I only have two arms. And if Enzo wouldn't kill me, I'd scoop Malachi up in one and Xavier in the other.

Cora clings to Jenna and Joseph stares longingly at the kitchen.

I only have two arms.

My heart cuts in half as I turn from them all and walk out the front door.

Alone.

FOURTEEN

Nick

As soon as the door closes behind me, I find Dane and Enzo in a heated discussion between their cars. Dane is visibly upset and Enzo is trying to calm him down.

"That was fucking torture," I growl, my eyes feeling watery after seeing those kids in person.

"I know," they both say at once.

Enzo sighs and clutches both our shoulders. "The day after Christmas, we see the judge. We'll do what we can."

"Thank you," Dane says to Enzo. "Thank you for all you do. You should come over and have dinner with us one night."

Enzo's brows lift as he looks over at me and then to Dane. "You're together?"

After tonight, I don't care about my dad or my job or the fact Dane's my boss. I don't care that I'm not doing the career I want or that my dad pushes me around sometimes. I don't care that my mom and sister are no longer individuals but something fake Dad has created. I don't care that I'm not normally a relationship guy. None of that matters.

"We're together," I agree, taking Dane's hand in mine.

Enzo smiles. "Yeah, I'll come for dinner one night. See you in court."

We wave to him and climb in the car. Once we're driving, I yank off my cap and beard, then close my eyes and think. Dane is quiet beside me, and it isn't until we've pulled into his garage and are getting out that either of us speaks. Dane pushes open the door into the house and closes it behind me.

"Those kids," is all he says.

I think of Xavier's words, and they replay over and over again in my head.

I don't want anyone to hurt my big brother and me.

"I want to help them. Why is it so hard to help them?" I choke out, hating that I'm so weak. These kids have dealt with so much more and they stand

162

there with their shoulders squared, wearing matching brave faces. I wish I were brave like them.

You can be.

My heart thumps at that idea. I can be brave. It starts small but I can do this. I'm already doing this with Dane. I'm changing the life my dad has molded for me into something I want for myself.

I want Dane.

"I'm going to quit," I tell him softly as he walks into the kitchen.

He stops and whirls around. "What?"

"After their case is over, I'm quitting."

"Why?" His gray eyes flash with hurt.

I walk over to him and kiss his mouth. He's the one pouting now, and it's a hot look on him. "Not us," I clarify with a smile. "I can't be an attorney anymore. It's not what I want to do."

His hands find my hips and he walks me until my back hits the fridge. Our mouths mate in a sweet, addictive way until we're both panting. "I'll hire you again."

I laugh. "I don't want to be an attorney. You can certainly try and persuade me, but it won't work."

He bites on my bottom lip in a playful way before reaching down to cup me through my Santa suit.

"Like this? Is this working?"

I groan when my dick hardens up. His naughty grin doesn't help the state of my cock. Dane is hotter when he's up to no good.

"That's pretty convincing," I say with a grunt.

"Would it be more convincing from my knees?" he asks with an arched brow.

"Most definitely."

He drops to one knee, still dressed in his coat that's covered in snow. As he pulls down the red velvet Santa slacks and then my gray sweats, I admire this man before me. Not just for his bedroom prowess. Not for how distinguished he appears with his older, more refined, looks. Not even for his fire-inducing smiles. I admire the man on the inside. The compassionate, driven, thoughtful, determined man. The one who somehow found the courage to go after this thing with us despite being worried about the outcome. His first shot at it was a fiasco with his best friend. The second time had to have been hard. But he did it anyway. And now, each day we're together, I see him fighting for it. He wants it so badly. He fights for us. He fights for *me*, dammit.

Dane is protective and nurturing, somehow in the same man. Something my father would never be capable of being. Dane is a thousand times more man than that of my father. I've never known another man like Dane. I've never been so gutted at the thought of losing someone before, and the very idea of this being some sort of fling kills me.

"We're not a fling," I tell him huskily as he pulls my cock from my boxers.

"No, we're not," he agrees, stroking me expertly. "We're much more. We always were."

Our eyes are locked as he jacks his fist up and down my dick slowly. Pleasure coils in the pit of my stomach, but it's what takes root inside my chest that has me pausing. Dane. He's there. Inside my heart, making a motherfucking home. My sad, impenetrable heart has been breached. This man before me has burrowed his way inside and doesn't seem keen on ever leaving.

"You think…" I trail off and hiss when his tongue teases my tip. "You think we're the 'forever' type of guys?"

His grin is crooked and hot as hell. "I think we are."

"What makes you so sure?"

He licks my tip again. "Because I've never felt like this before."

With those words, his lips slide down my cock, taking me deep in his throat. My fingers find his hair and I grip it, closing my eyes, as I get lost to the way he sucks me off. His groans rumble down my shaft and make my balls ache for release. When he pushes deeper and swallows the head of my cock down his hot throat, making a gagging sound in the process, I come abruptly and without warning.

"Fuck!" I roar. "Fuck, D."

He swallows my release and pulls away before standing. When our lips are a breath away, he tenderly strokes my cheek. This man is affectionate and I crave his touch. I've never needed something so simple in all my life.

"I was married to Janice for a long time," he tells me, his hot stare piercing mine. "But not once, not even on our wedding night or when our daughter was born, did I ever feel for that woman what I feel for you. I felt more from you the moment you smiled at me than my entire marriage with her. I don't think you quite get it, Nick. This thing between us is strong and unbreakable. I know you hate labels and calling a spade a spade, but this is love, babe."

His words cut through to my heart and I feel as though I'm hemorrhaging. I want to believe in what he says, but is my life that easy? Do I finally get something I've desperately craved so deep in my soul?

I'm frozen, unable to speak, when he gives me a soft smile.

"I'm getting rid of our useless IT guy. He never comes to work half the time anyway. We need someone who knows what the hell they're doing. Will you accept the job, Nick? You're the only one I want for it."

My heart thumps. "I thought you'd never ask, boss."

His eyes gleam wickedly. "Now it's time for you to thank me for my generosity."

I start to lower but he shakes his head.

"You know I prefer your ass," he says in a deep, husky tone. "Besides, it's about time for Santa to sit on someone else's lap for a change. If you're a good boy and ride my dick like you own it, I'll let you come."

A chuckle escapes me. "You're hot as fuck when you're bossy."

"Fuck," I groan as I ease down his thickness. Straddling him on the couch and while we kiss has got to be the hottest fuck we've ever had. What's even hotter is the

feral way with which he grabs my ass cheeks, spreading me further apart to take his impressive cock.

"Feels good, hmmm?" he rumbles against my lips. His grip on my dick is maddening as he pleasures me.

"So good."

My ass clenches when I get close to coming. Based on his ragged breathing, he's close too. Our fucking becomes frantic—his hips thrusting up as I grind on him. Soon, we're both groaning as our orgasms tremor through us. His cock throbs inside me as my cum shoots against his bare chest.

"That good, huh?" Dane asks from the driver's seat, dragging me from the memory of last night after our shower.

I give him a shrug. "Don't tell me you're not still thinking about it. That shit was hot as hell. Admit it."

He chuckles. "It was fucking fantastic."

The rest of the drive to Mel's is filled with light conversation and laughter. When we arrive, we park behind a bright red Mercedes. Dane's entire demeanor changes upon seeing the car. Must be Janice.

We get out of the car and he opens the hatch. I grab the crate of food while he picks up the one with the presents. As we approach the nice suburban home, my nerves start to fray. What if his daughter doesn't like me?

He's assured me that she will but I'm still nervous. She's only known her dad with her mother. How will she feel knowing he's not only seeing someone, but a guy at that?

She'll have to get over it because I'm not going anywhere.

The new thought calms my nerves and I follow him inside the house. Upon entering, we're met with the scent of ham and other delicious smells. I'm re-laxed right into a smile. Mel—the same beautiful young woman from the pictures at Dane's—catches me grinning.

"Ahhh, you must be Nick. Dad said he'd be bring-ing you," she greets as she leans in to kiss my cheek. "Merry Christmas, Daddy." She gives him a side hug and he kisses the top of her head.

"Merry Christmas, sweetheart. Where's Stan?" Dane asks.

"In the kitchen. He and Mom are arguing over the caloric content of sweet potato casserole. Last I heard, he was trying to convince her it was fat-free," Mel says with a chuckle.

Dane laughs and sets the crate down on the floor, then turns to pull some food from my crate. I follow them into the kitchen, where his ex-wife stands next to a tall, wiry red-headed guy who wears the nerdiest pair of glasses on his freckled nose. Like Mel, Janice is beautiful, with the same dark brown hair as her daughter. It surprises me Mel would be with such a nerdy guy.

"I'm not eating it, Stan," Janice says, pouting.

He shrugs. "But you'd be missing out on the best fat-free sweet potato casserole in the world. Yolo, J. Yolo."

She gives him a playful shove. "Fine. I'll have a bite." When Janice turns and sees me, her eyes widen in surprise. "Who do we have here?"

Dane walks over to Janice and kisses her cheek. "Merry Christmas. Where's your date?" He ignores her question altogether.

She straightens and arches a perfect brow. "Oh, Damien? He's watching a football game in the living room." She gives him the fakest smile ever. "Damien used to play pro basketball."

Dane, uncaring, shakes Stan's hand before gesturing at me. "This is my date," he says, as though it's the most natural thing in the world. "Nicholas Stratton."

Janice makes a choking sound. "Your what?"

"Mother," Mel warns. "Daddy's seeing Nick." Mel shoots me a warm stare. It's then I realize she must have already known. With her and Dane being so close, it makes sense he may have already told her.

"But he's a…" She trails off, her face pinched into a horrified expression.

Stan saves the day. "A guy? A hot one too. Dane has good taste."

She can't argue with that since she was married to him. "Oh." Then she scowls. "Is this why our marriage didn't work?"

Dane laughs. "No, it didn't work because we weren't compatible. But we made one helluva perfect kid."

Mel preens in the kitchen and, just like that, the tense moment is gone. I get roped into stirring corn on the stove for Stan while Dane is forced to cut the ham. Janice flits about the kitchen, making comments here and there, while Mel pulls items out of the fridge. The elusive Damien—a giant black man with a handsome face but a sour attitude—pokes his head in a time or two. Eventually, we all sit down to dinner.

It's messy and loud and chaotic.

People say the wrong things and snort with laughter and jab insults.

My mother would be horrified.

And I've never felt so at home.

FIFTEEN

Dane

Oh, Janice.

Being around her for the first time in weeks is a reminder why we divorced in the first place. It had nothing to do with my secretly being gay. I faked it for her. I tried for her. I did everything in my power to make it work for her because we had Mel, and she was such a perfect product of something I didn't entirely want for myself. It made the decision to marry a woman, despite my heart's desires, all worth it. The moment Janice told me she was pregnant, I was elated. I loved that little bean from the second I knew about her.

But I never loved Janice.

I loved her as the mother of my child and as a partner in our life, but never that soul-wrenching and deep, crushing type of love. Frankly, I didn't know that type of love existed. The only person I'd felt love for was Max. And it was unrequited. But even back then, my heart didn't ache with such need and passion and desire as it does now. The way it does with Nick.

My gaze falls on Nick from across the table. Stan is showing him something on his phone and Nick is nodding. Stan's a tech nerd too, so I'm glad they seem to be interested in something common. Mel keeps chattering to Damien about God only knows what. That girl could carry on a conversation with a tree. Damien is a big-ass, grumpy tree, but even he can't resist her charms. I catch him smiling a time or two for her. As for me, I'm stuck listening to Janice tell me about how she's decided to become a personal trainer. I nod at her but I'm distracted again by Nick. He watches me intently from across the table, the same emotions bubbling inside me reflecting in his brown eyes.

I wish I were sitting beside him. The urge to touch him often is overwhelming. I can't get him out of my head and I certainly don't want him gone. I want him infecting my every thought.

His lips curl up on one side in a lazy grin. The same lazy grin that had me following him up to his hotel room that night. Back then, he'd seemed like such a carefree guy without a worry in the world. Little did I know, he had enough worries for the both of us combined.

He winks at me and Janice huffs in frustration beside me.

"You're not listening." Her lips pout out and her nostrils flare.

"Sorry," I grumble.

She leans in and clutches my bicep with her pointy fingernails. "I think it's weird, Dane. Friend to friend."

Tensing at her words, I shoot her a glare. "It's not really any of your business."

The rest of the table is loud with conversation, so our private one goes unheard. I do feel Nick's stare on us, though.

"I just worry about you," she says, in that fake tone of hers that used to grate on my nerves. Turns out, it still does.

"Well, don't," I grunt.

"Have you slept with him? How do you know you're even into that sort of thing? You're an excellent lover with women. Do you even know how to have sex with a guy?" she hisses, her fingernails poking harder through my sweater.

"That is *absolutely* none of your business. But if you must know, Nick and I manage just fine." I grit my teeth and glower at her.

"Nick and I," she parrots, her voice condescending in tone. "You're already a thing, huh? I mean, you're so much older, and he's Mel's age, for crying out loud. How long do you think this little tryst will last, Dane?"

"Mother," Mel says in a sharp voice, reprimanding Janice.

"No," Janice retorts, loud enough for everyone to hear. "It needs to be said. What kind of family are we if we don't protect your poor father?"

"I don't need prot—"

Janice cuts me off. "Oh, sweetie, stop. Mel and I have discussed how far off the deep end you've fallen since I filed for divorce. Now that it's finalized, you've gone off and done something crazy." She shoots a pointed look at Nick.

"Mother!" Mel shrieks, and then flashes me a pleading stare. "Daddy, we most certainly didn't discuss this."

"You're not gay, Dane," Janice bites out. "There, I said it. You were married to me for twenty-six years and we had a child together. You've had your face be-tween my thighs. Certainly didn't seem very gay then."

Damien pulls her wine glass from her other hand, and has the sense to appear ashamed by her words. Nick clenches his jaw and fists his hand on the table.

"We're not talking about this over Christmas din-ner," I say calmly, trying desperately not to cut Mel's mother down in front of her.

"I can't believe you," Mel mutters to her mother. "Must you always do this to him?"

"Why am I the villain here?" Janice bellows. "I'm always the villain because I don't live in a fantasy world. Not everything is rainbows and sunshine." She sneers at Nick. "Well, maybe rainbows for you."

"Janice," I growl out in warning. "That's enough."

"I'm just saying—"

"Nobody cares what you have to 'just say,'" Nick barks out, rising from his seat. "You're a drunk mean girl in an old woman's body. Get ahold of your-self. You're embarrassing everyone here, but mostly yourself."

"Excuse me?" Janice shrieks.

"Oh God," Mel groans.

"Guys," Stan tries to placate.

I pinch the bridge of my nose, hating the

awkwardness of another one of Janice's bash-fests. So often, I want to tell her what a bitch she is but it already hurts Mel enough hearing it from one parent. She doesn't need it from both.

"I love him and he loves me."

I snap my head up and lock eyes with Nick. His brown-eyed stare is filled with so many emotions.

Silence falls on the table as my eyes rake down my man. He's strong and young and beautiful. And mine.

I love him and he loves me.

"You may not understand what's transpired between us, Janice, but it doesn't change the fact that it has. I'm sorry, but this has nothing to do with the past or your marriage to him. It has everything to do with what we can give to each other." Nick smiles at me as he continues, his words meant for Janice. "Your marriage didn't work because something was missing. Just like every relationship I've ever had fail too. We hadn't found each other and now that we have, it'd do you some good to accept that your daughter's father has found love. I can bet money that it makes her happy. It'd make her even happier if you'd respect her father and back the fuck off."

Stan snorts and Damien mutters under his

breath. Mel nods from beside me.

"Let it rest, Mom," she says, her voice softening. "Please."

Janice shifts in her seat and then utters out an apology. It's quiet but it's there. And since I've known her since college, I know it's genuine.

"Thank you. Now Janice, did you make my pie or what?" I tease, trying to lighten the mood.

She laughs. "Divorced or not, Christmas wouldn't be Christmas without my homemade pecan pie. Even if I can't eat it this year," she grumbles.

Damien takes her hand. "Eat the pie, Jan."

"Well, if you insist," she huffs. "When I gain five pounds from looking at it, and another ten from the first bite, you're the one who'll have to deal with it."

Damien shrugs. "I like my women thick."

"Since when?" she asks, horrified.

"Since now."

Nick leans against me on the couch, his arm posses-sively hung over my shoulders. It should feel strange or awkward displaying our affection to everyone, but it doesn't. I had imagined feeling embarrassed or shy over the fact that I'm openly gay. But that shame nev-er came. Pride surges through me to have this man at my side. I love how possessive and protective he is.

I love him and he loves me.

Mel hands me a glass of hot cocoa spiked with brandy. I chuckle when she plops down in Stan's lap and forces him to drink some. He makes a face but eventually gives in. They're such a mismatched pair but they somehow work. I've been so distracted by Nick and my own issues that I'm just now noticing the tremor in Mel's hand. Stan covers it with his, immedi-ately relaxing her. Right then, I pray to every god out there that he holds on and never lets her go.

"We have an announcement," Stan says, shooting a look my way.

I give him a nod. We met up for drinks months ago when he asked for her hand in marriage. I'd obliged but he never has pulled the trigger. Or so I'd thought. I see now that she's wearing a simple band on her finger. Not an engagement ring, but a wedding ring.

Oh, shit.

Janice is going to lose her mind.

"We got married back in September when we went to Cozumel," Mel blurts out. Her panicked eyes meet mine and I smile at her. She relaxes but chews on her bottom lip.

"I thought you went there for business," Janice says, her voice shrill.

"We did, but then decided to just go ahead and get married. I never wanted a big wedding. Just Stan and I."

He nods, pride shining in his eyes. "It was perfect, just the two of us."

"But your dress? And you didn't want your dad to walk you down the aisle? A big wedding is every girl's dream," Janice chokes out, close to tears.

"Not mine," Mel tells her. "My dream was to find love. I found it." She sighs and her bottom lip trembles. "But that's not what our announcement is."

"You're pregnant," Janice hisses.

Mel shakes her head and tears well in her eyes. Stan scowls at Janice.

"I'm sterile," Stan says in a sad tone. "We learned that recently."

The room falls quiet, and I see Janice's cheeks turn pink.

"We're going to adopt," Mel tells us, her smile once again returning. "We're excited to bring a child into our home. We've already begun the process."

I rise from the sofa and walk over to Mel. When I pull her up and into a hug, she clutches me hard.

"Thank you for not freaking out. If I would have had a wedding, of course you'd have walked me down the aisle."

I chuckle and smooth out her hair with my palm before kissing the top of her head. "Of course," I agree. "I'm proud of you. I'm happy you found Stan, and I'm proud of you two for your decision to adopt."

"Thanks, Daddy. I love you."

"Love you too, sweetheart."

Stan stands up and pulls Mel back into his arms. Love glitters in her eyes as she stares up at him as though he's the best man in the entire world. As her dad, I should feel heartache that my baby girl looks at someone else as though they hang the moon. But I couldn't be prouder.

"Congrats, son," I say, offering my hand to him. "I'm glad she's into nerds."

He snorts. "No shit."

SIXTEEN

Nick

Enzo: Where are you?

I glance down at my phone, but don't reply because I'm running down the corridor to the courtroom. Dane and I stayed up way too late last night consumed by one another. This morning, he had to meet with a client and I overslept. Of course, I overslept on the worst possible day. I'd barely had time to brush my teeth, throw on a suit, and grab my bag before I was running out the door. I had to put my tie on in the car and forgo coffee altogether.

Eventually, I make it to the courtroom and push inside. The room hushes and I keep my gaze diverted to the floor as I rush to the front. I find Enzo and sit beside him.

"So glad you could make it," a familiar voice deadpans.

I jerk my head up and lock with a pair of green eyes. Max Rowe. Fuck. He's at the bench, a gavel resting in front of him, dressed in a black robe. His eyes are narrowed and he seems annoyed by my presence.

"I apologize, Your Honor."

He picks up a pair of black-rimmed reading glasses and sits them on the end of his nose as he looks over a file. We spend the next half hour on edge, as Max drills us with questions and wants clarification on parts of the reports. By the end of it, I'm feeling doubtful.

"Permission to approach the bench," I utter.

Max narrows his eyes at me but then gives me a clipped nod. I rise from my seat and stride over to the podium. His jaw clenches as he regards me with scrutiny. As though I'm not good enough to be an attorney—I'm not. As though I'm not good enough to be Dane's—I am.

"The little guy, Xavier," I say softly. "He asked Santa for him and his brother not to be hurt anymore."

Max's gaze softens slightly. "Everything checks out here." He thumps the paper.

"It does…" I trail off, feeling defeated. Then I

remember the steely strength in those boys' gray eyes. "But sometimes what's on the surface isn't always right."

He cocks his head slightly as he watches me. "I agree."

"There are some other places that have been checked and verified. Safer places. All we're asking is to get them moved," I tell him.

"I'm sorry, counselor, but I don't think that's all you're asking. I feel like you're asking a lot more than even I'm able to give." He frowns and my heart sinks. "But something tells me you're the kind of guy who finds a way to get what he wants anyway. For the life of me, I don't want to help you…for my own reasons. But I will. I'll grant all five children to be placed in one of the proposed homes."

I gape at him, my heart thudding. "Really?"

"Something tells me that won't be enough, though."

"For now, it will be. Thank you, Your Honor."

The gavel slams down and I feel like I've won.

On so many levels.

Two months later...

"Are you sure I'm welcome?" I ask as Dane pulls his Porsche into Max's driveway. "The guy doesn't exactly like me."

He scoffs. "Dorian does. She wears the pants."

I roll my eyes but can't help but chuckle. Dorian has the most issues with computers at the firm. I swear she breaks them on purpose just so she can show me pictures of her son. When I'd confessed about my run-in with Max at the bar, where I nearly kicked his ass over Dane, she just laughed and told me everything was going to be okay.

I hope she's right.

We climb out and it's cold as fuck outside. Snow is fun during Christmas but when it's February and still snowing, it's no longer fun. It's annoying. I rush into the house behind Dane and am immediately tense at the similar type of house my parents live in. The foyer is ornate and fancy. I'm at unease until we walk into the living room. Pictures line every wall and corner. Max's daughters sit on the couch with Dorian. When Dorian sees me, she jumps up and rushes over to us and I'm immediately welcomed in her hug.

"I'm so glad you came, Nick," she says. "Don't worry. Max doesn't hold grudges long."

Dane chuckles. "Where's Max?"

"In the kitchen with the boys," she replies. "Come on. You need to meet my step daughters."

Both women are gorgeous—a spitting image of their father. The one I learn is named Olivia is bubbly and always smiling. Soph, the younger one, frowns a lot. She has a suspicious glint in her green eyes that rivals her father's.

"You're Uncle Dane's *friend*?" Soph asks once I settle in a chair across from them. Her words are cold and accusatory. Maybe *she* should be a goddamn attorney.

"Boyfriend," I clarify, meeting her hard stare.

Olivia grins. "I knew it. I knew he was into guys."

Soph frowns at her before turning back to me. "Is it serious or is this some sort of fling?"

"Soph," Dorian warns gently.

"I love him," I tell her proudly. "And he loves me."

My words soften her right up because she graces me with a pretty smile. "Well, that's settled then. I heard you're good with computers. Can you fix my iPad?"

"For fifty bucks," I tease.

"Never mind that price. I'll take it to the Apple store."

"And they'll fuck it up real good for you," I tell her smugly.

Her lip curls up. "Fine." Then she hollers, "Drew! I need fifty bucks!"

A deep "No" resounds from the kitchen.

She flips him off, even though he can't see her. "Do it for free, and I won't poison your food when you're not looking."

I arch a brow at her and both Olivia and Dorian snigger. "Damn, you're cold," I retort.

She smiles sweetly at me. "Do we have a deal?"

"It sounds an awful lot like extortion. Don't make me call my lawyer." I shoot Dorian a knowing look.

Dorian laughs. "If I'm going to be your lawyer instead of Dane, then you need to figure out a new payment plan. I can assure you I don't accept whatever form of payment he does."

Olivia snorts and Soph gives me a wicked grin.

"How about you keep your dad from killing me and I'll fix all your computer problems for the rest of your life?" I hold my hand out to Soph.

She eyes it like it's a snake. "You're in this for life?"

I think of the way Dane makes me so fucking

happy. All the time. Whether it's at home or at the office or in bed. Always.

"I am," I agree.

She shakes my hand. "You got yourself a deal, nerd."

Once again, I'm sitting at a lively dinner table and my heart beats wildly in my chest. I wish I could bring Christina. My sister could use the break from the monotony that is our cold, boring home. I text her here and there to check on her, but she's busy with her own life. I can tell she's Team Dad because she doesn't give me elaborated answers. It's enough though, knowing she's doing okay without me.

I quickly learn that Miles worships the ground Olivia walks on. He watches her like he wants to eat her. Max and Dorian are like a milder, older version of them. But it's Soph and Drew who are the entertaining ones. She gives him shit and he gives it right back. They spend the entire dinner arguing but something tells me—by the twinkle in her eye and the barely hidden smug grin of his—that this is their foreplay. Babies get passed around and at one point, I have two in my arms.

A pang slices through my heart.

I only have two arms.

My mood sours as I worry about Malachi and Xavier. Enzo says they're doing okay, but I can't help but worry. He confessed he's more worried about Jenna. She turns eighteen soon and will be forced from the system. Cora loves her and it's going to be hard on them both. It's still a sad story. At least one of them is getting his happily ever after.

"Mel and Stan are adopting a boy named Joseph," Dane tells Olivia. "A lot of red tape, but your dad is helping make that happen."

Olivia beams at her father, so proud of him. In this moment, despite my beef with the guy, I'm proud too. He really did us a solid with those kids. When Mel mentioned adopting, Dane and I were quick to help. Turns out, they fell in love with little Joseph upon meeting him. They're still going through the rigorous amounts of paperwork but within a few weeks, it'll be a done deal.

"Tell her to bring him by," Dorian says to Dane. "We'd love to meet the little guy."

The rest of dinner goes well, but my mind is stuck on the Bryant boys. My heart aches for them. So much that I slip out of the dining room and into an office so I can text Enzo.

Me: How are my boys?

Enzo: They're doing fine. I wish I could say the same for Cora and Jenna.

Me: What's wrong?

Enzo: Jenna just thinks it's as simple as her adopting Cora when she turns eighteen. She has no job. No income. Struggling in school. It's not that easy.

Me: Nothing ever is.

I rub at the tension on the back of my neck as I wait for him to respond. Looking around, I realize I'm in Max's office. Books line every shelf. Pictures sit in every empty spot. It's warm and inviting in here.

Enzo: She's going to be heartbroken.

Me: How do you do this job, man?

Enzo: The job does me. The job is a cruel bitch.

Almost immediately, he texts again.

Enzo: I will do what I can, sweetheart. You know this.

I frown in confusion.

Me: Sweetheart?

Enzo: Sorry. Wrong person.

"Snooping, huh?" Max asks from the doorway.

I flinch and pocket my phone. "Just texting Enzo. I'm worried about the Bryant boys." Honesty always is the best policy.

He crosses his arms over his chest and regards me with an unreadable expression. "I didn't get it that night."

I cock my head to the side, waiting for him to continue.

"You. Dane. I didn't understand what was happening." He sighs and scrubs his palm across his scruffy cheek. "I just didn't want my best friend to get hurt. And here this cocky little sonofabitch was, in my face, yelling at me for shit that I thought I'd long since buried."

I grit my teeth. "Pain doesn't disappear with time. You hurt him."

He nods. "I realize that. Hell, I knew it at the time. I was embarrassed and confused as to why he'd do that. I'm ashamed of how I reacted. When you're in your early twenties, you think differently than when you're older. I never wanted to hurt Dane. I love him like a brother." He walks over to a shelf where a picture of him and Dane sits. They're both wearing graduation gowns and look much younger. "When you were up in my face, I was pissed. Stewed over that conversation for days. Then, when I saw you in the courtroom, I got mad all over again."

I'm thankful as hell he didn't allow his anger at me cloud his judgment.

"But then I saw your passion once again. You're a fighter, Nick. You fight for those around you who don't seem to know they need fighting for. I saw it in your eyes as you fought for those kids. I see it now, how you fight for Dane." He smiles at me, and it's beautiful and genuine. Apparently, this guy is likable and I'm the only one who didn't like him. "You're good for him. I've never seen him so happy."

"Dane's worth fighting for," I tell him. "Those kids are too."

He winks at me. "Keep fighting. I'm on your side, buddy."

SEVENTEEN

Dane

Four months later…

Nick saunters out of the bathroom with just a towel hanging loosely around his hips. He's a picture of perfection. Solid, tanned muscles. A lean, young body. His brown hair is wet and hangs in a messy way over his eyebrows, giving him a roguish look. My gaze travels down his sculpted chest to the defined V in his lower abdomen. A V I've licked more times than I can count. If I could worship a letter of the alphabet, it'd be V.

He stops at the edge of the bed and smirks. "Enjoying the view, old man?"

"You know I am. Just thinking about getting that towel away from you and inside that tight ass of yours," I tell him, as though we're talking about the weather.

His cock flinches beneath the towel. "Who says it won't be me in your ass tonight?"

I sit up and tug off my T-shirt. "I was hoping we could sample a little of both. I'm extra hungry to-night." When I toss it at him, he laughs and then drops his towel. Our humor fades as he grabs the bottle of lube and climbs into bed with me. For a moment, we lie facing each other. His fingers run over my shoul-der as mine thread through his hair.

"Any regrets?" I ask, my voice husky and raw. I have none, but once I was sure, I was sure.

"I'm not exactly marriage material, but now you're stuck with me," he says with a grin. Despite his playful words, I hear the pain hidden in them. Still, even after all this time together, he doubts himself. It doesn't help that his father is a shitty human and continues to treat him like scum. Thank fuck his dad moved on to another law firm. I don't think either of us could continue working with him after all he's put Nick through. And thankfully, the temporary con-tract was just that. Temporary. At the end of the trial, he was gone.

"I married Janice," I tease. "Anything's a step up from that."

He growls and it only serves to make my dick

hard. "Fuck you, old man."

"You'll get your wish." I lean forward and kiss his pouty mouth. "I love you, and I knew who I married. I married you. And today was the best day of my life."

His body relaxes and we lose ourselves to a kiss. Today, we cut out of work early and went to the courthouse. In Max's office, with Dorian and Mel as our witnesses, Nick and I were married by Judge Rowe. Simple yet binding. I always knew he was mine. Now the law agrees with me.

"I can't shake the dread that one day, I'll fuck it all up," he admits, his voice hoarse with emotion.

I slide my leg between his thighs and kiss him hard, as though I can pour my reassurances right down his throat, into his heart. He groans when our dicks rub against each other. His is naked and mine is barely clothed by my boxers.

"You're not going to fuck it all up," I assure him. "I won't let you because I'll be there every step of the way."

He rolls me away from him, onto my stomach. He kisses his way down my back before grabbing the waistband of my boxers and tugging them down my thighs. Once I'm naked, he pours lube on his cock.

As he strokes it all over, I can hear the slick sounds

it makes. Then, his lubed fingers are sliding down my ass crack, sliding against my hole. He's a much more generous lover than I am. Always priming me to take him. Sometimes, I lose myself to the passion. It works though, because Nick gets off on a little pain.

His fingers are soon replaced with his cock. Slick and unsheathed. A tremor of excitement ripples through me. We'd gotten tested before marriage to make sure we were disease-free, and now that we both have the all-clear, I want nothing between us.

The burn as he prods my opening is always so intense at first. For a split-second, I always panic. But then, like now, he slides inside me and takes me to new heights of pleasure.

"Fuck," we both groan in unison.

Once he's fully seated inside me, he goes back to reverently kissing my shoulder. With his dick stretching my ass and my body pinned beneath his, I feel completely at his mercy. But I trust him fully. He's my husband.

"I love you," he murmurs, his hot breath against my flesh. "More than you will ever know."

Pleasure ripples through me when he begins a slow, sensual thrusting against me. I love that I can feel his skin and not the annoyance of a rubber between us. It's just us. Together, like we should be.

"Nick," I groan, my voice a raspy plea. "Fuck, I love you too."

He smiles against my skin and then nips at my flesh. "Mine," he growls.

His thrusting becomes hard and wild. I feel like he might be trying to split me in half so he can climb inside me. I want him there. I let him ravage me like he so desperately craves, and then his ragged breaths become moans. The sounds coming from him are so erotic that my cock spills and I soak the bed with my release. His heat floods inside me like a river. Hot and furious. I'd only imagined what it'd feel like to have nothing in between us, but I never thought it would feel this good. This possessive. I want to pin him down and fuck another release into his ass to claim him, but I can't deny how good it feels to be claimed by him too.

We're good together.

Really good.

His body is sweaty as he relaxes against me, his cock still twitching inside me. We'll both need a shower after this.

"Dane." My name on his lips comes out broken. "I want more than this."

"More?"

"Do you ever wish you would have had more kids?"

Long ago, I'd broached the subject with Janice about giving Mel a sibling. She shot me down and told me her body barely recovered from giving birth once, and she sure as hell wasn't going through that again.

"Yeah," I admit.

"I want kids." His cock twitches inside me.

I chuckle. "Unfortunately, we can't have any."

He slides out and his cum runs down, drenching my balls. I roll onto my back and he settles against my chest. You'd think two hard, muscled bodies wouldn't fit together comfortably. We seem to always cuddle just fine. His brown eyes are sad and serious.

"We can, though," he says. "You know we can."

He means through adoption. Seeing Stan and Mel with Joseph has been beautiful to watch. Even Janice has turned into a doting grandma. They brought such joy into that child's life. Nick and I have the power to do that too.

"How are the Bryant boys?" I ask, knowing he and Enzo are friends now. Enzo keeps him in the loop.

"They're okay, but I think they'd be happier if they were Alexanders."

"I think you're right," I agree, stroking his messy hair out of his eyes. "You're sure about this?"

"I've never been so sure about anything besides you." His mouth presses to mine and he kisses me as though he must convince me. Too bad he already convinced me to give him whatever he wants the second he smiled at me at that office Christmas party. Lucky for him, I want it too. I feel like I've been given a second chance at life. This time, I get to dictate how it goes. I'd never trade Mel in for a second, but I'm happy as hell to have this shot at a new path.

"Let's do this," I murmur against his full lips. "Let's find a way to get our boys."

"Our boys."

Six months later…

"Stop pacing," I instruct. "You're going to freak them out."

Nick pauses and runs his fingers through his hair. "What if they don't like us? What if they don't want to live with us?"

I grab his hand and squeeze. "But what if they

do? Besides, it's too late to go back. We're doing this."

This seems to settle his mind because he relaxes. When Enzo walks in with both boys on either side of him, my nerves hitch too. They're bigger than I remember. Still cute as ever. Both of them seem just as nervous as us.

Enzo gives them each a gentle squeeze on the shoulders and bends down to whisper something to them. They grin and it stops my heart.

"I'm Dane and this is Nick," I tell them, dropping to one knee. "Do you remember me?"

Malachi nods his head and then looks at Nick as though he remembers him too. Xavier is smaller, so he probably doesn't recognize us.

"I'm Malachi," he says as he approaches, dragging his brother behind. "This is Xavier."

Nick kneels down beside me and smiles at them. "You're going to love your new house," he assures them. "This guy saved me when my dad was beating me up. He let me come live with him. He was already a good dad to his daughter, Mel. Do you remember Joseph? He went to live with Mel."

Both boys smile.

"Can we see him again?" Xavier asks.

"Of course," Nick says. "Dane was such a good

dad that he taught his daughter Mel how to be a good mom. Joseph is safe with her. She's nice, and his new dad Stan makes food all the time. Joseph is never hungry."

"He really loves macaroni and cheese," I tell them. "And ice cream."

The boys seem to be warming up. The hopeful look in their eyes makes my heart clench.

"Dane was such a good dad," Nick says, "that he taught me to be a good dad too. He taught me how to be safe. I never want to be like my dad. I want to be good to my kids."

Both kids watch him with wide eyes. Curious and unsure.

"Two Christmases ago, I wrote a letter and asked Santa for something really special," he tells them. "I wished that he'd let me be a good dad. He wrote me back and told me about two special boys who didn't have a dad. They were sad and people hurt them. I wanted to protect them and make them happy."

The boys listen with rapt attention. Pride surges through me at how good Nick is with them.

"He told me that the boys were too special. That one dad wasn't enough for them. For all the sad times they went through, they deserved two dads," he says, smiling at me.

"We get two dads?" Xavier asks in awe.

Nick pretends to flex a muscle. "Two strong dads for two strong boys."

Xavier shows his non-existent muscle as Malachi giggles. They're cute and funny. Their personalities are hiding under fear and uncertainty. With time, we'll pull them out of their shells and help them see they don't have to be afraid any longer.

"I hope you boys like food too," I say to them. "Joseph's mom and dad filled up our cabinets with foods Joseph was just sure you would love."

"Really?" Malachi asks, as though he can't truly believe it.

"Really."

Xavier rushes into my arms and throws his arms around my neck. I squeeze him tight. Malachi looks at Nick like maybe he might want a hug too, so I nudge Nick.

He opens his arms and Malachi falls into them.

Nick and I exchange glances. His brown eyes shine with happiness, a perfect mirror to mine.

EPILOGUE

Nick

Christmas Day...

"Look, Daddy," Xavier cries out in his cute froggy voice, waving a box of Legos at me from the floor. "Santa knew I wanted this!"

I rub the sleep out of my eyes and yawn. "Santa knows everything."

Xavier giggles and then sets to opening another present. Malachi is leaned up against me. He's a sleepyhead like me. Xavier and Dane are the morning people in our house.

"You going to open your presents?" I ask my oldest son.

"I want to sit with you, Dad, and watch Xavier open his," he says quietly.

I give him a little squeeze and kiss the top of his head. "Okay, bub."

With one son in my arms and the other grinning from ear to ear on the floor, I can't help but realize life has a plan. Even the sad kids with shitty parents sometimes get their happy endings. These boys did. As did Joseph. Hell, even me. Jenna and Cora's was a little harder to come by, but even those angels found love in an unexpected place. But that's a story for another day…

Dane exits the kitchen with two mugs of coffee. He earns a smile for being my savior this morning, and this morning, he's looking extra fine in full-on dad mode. He's wearing flannel pajama bottoms and his favorite grandpa slippers. It's his T-shirt the boys gave him last night that makes me happy. The same one I'm wearing: Super Dad.

He hands me a mug and then sits down on the floor beside Xavier. They talk about his presents and how we'll go see Joseph later today. Both boys think it's hilarious that they're uncles to their friend. Joseph refuses to call them Uncle Malachi and Uncle Xavier, and instead insists they call him Uncle Joseph.

Eventually, Malachi perks up and joins his brother on the floor. Dane stands and stretches before settling on the couch beside me. He takes my hand and squeezes it.

Had I known the night I stared at the hot older man from across the bar would lead to this, I'd have kissed him right then and proposed marriage. Not sure he'd have accepted, though. I had to coax him into my bed. Then, he never wanted to leave.

As if cued into my thoughts, he turns and flashes me a devilish grin. "What are you smirking about?"

I shrug. "Just thinking about the night we met."

"I'm glad you found me," he says, his gray eyes twinkling.

"Took some convincing, though."

"I was worth it," he jokes.

He has no idea.

Leaning forward, I rest my forehead against his. "You're still worth it."

He plants a kiss on my cheek and then his mouth finds my ear. "Are you flirting with me, Mr. Alexander?"

"Perhaps."

We share a long stare filled with heat and emotion and love.

Until we're attacked by two little rugrats. Our boys are as affectionate as their fathers. They fell right into this family the same way Dane and I fell into love. Quickly. Perfectly. As though it was always meant to be.

The boys babble about their stockings and cookies and snow. They talk about the *Star Wars* movies and Legos and XBOX. There are giggles and snorts and jokes. Smiles and hugs.

And love.

A love that just keeps on growing.

I may only have two arms…but they're big, and all three of my boys fit inside. Who knows…maybe one day, there will be room for a few more.

Dane winks at me.

He hopes so.

I hope so too.

The End

If you loved *Dane*,
you'll love his best friend's story in *Malfeasance*!

K Webster's Taboo World

Cast of Characters

Brandt Smith (Rick's Best Friend)
Kelsey McMahon (Rick's Daughter)
Rick McMahon (Sheriff)
Mandy Halston (Kelsey's Best Friend)

Miles Reynolds (Drew's Best Friend)
Olivia Rowe (Max's Daughter/Sophia's Sister)

Dane Alexander (Max's Best Friend)
Nick Stratton

Judge Maximillian "Max" Rowe (Olivia and Sophia's Father)
Dorian Dresser

Drew Hamilton (Miles's Best Friend)
Sophia Rowe (Max's Daughter/Olivia's Sister)

Easton McAvoy (Preacher)
Lacy Greenwood (Stephanie's Daughter)

Stephanie Greenwood (Lacy's Mother)
Anthony Blakely (Quinn's Son)
Aiden Blakely (Quinn's Son)

Quinn Blakely (Anthony and Aiden's Father)
Ava Prince (Lacy/Raven/Olivia's friend)

Karelma Bonilla (Mateo's Daughter)
Adam Renner (Principal)

Coach Everett Long (Adam's friend)
River Banks (Olivia's Best Friend)

Mateo Bonilla (Four Fathers Series Side Character)

Vaughn Young
Vale Young

K Webster's Taboo World Reading List

These don't necessarily have to be read in order to enjoy, but if you would like to know the order I wrote them in, it is as follows (with more being added to as I publish):

Bad Bad Bad
Coach Long
Ex-Rated Attraction
Mr. Blakely
Malfeasance
Easton (Formerly known as Preach)
Crybaby
Lawn Boys
Renner's Rules
The Glue
*Dane (*Beginning of story from *What Happens During the Holidays Anthology)*

Books by K Webster

TABOO TREATS:
Bad Bad Bad—BANNED (only sold on K Webster's website)
Coach Long
Easton
Crybaby
Lawn Boys
Malfeasance
Renner's Rules
The Glue
Dane

CARINA PRESS BOOKS:
Ex-Rated Attraction
Mr. Blakely
Bidding for Keeps

FOUR FATHERS BOOKS:
Pearson

FOUR SONS BOOKS:
Camden

Standalone Novels:

Apartment 2B

Love and Law

Moth to a Flame

Erased

The Road Back to Us

Surviving Harley

Give Me Yesterday

Running Free

Dirty Ugly Toy

Zeke's Eden

Sweet Jayne

Untimely You

Mad Sea

Whispers and the Roars

Schooled by a Senior

B-Sides and Rarities

Blue Hill Blood by Elizabeth Gray

Notice

The Wild—BANNED (only sold on K Webster's website)

The Day She Cried

My Torin

El Malo

Sunshine and the Stalker

Sundays are for Hangovers

Hale

ACKNOWLEDGEMENTS

Thank you to my husband. You make me smile every single day! I love you bunches!

A huge thank you to my Krazy for K Webster's Books reader group. You all are insanely supportive and I can't thank you enough.

A gigantic thank you to those who always help me out. Elizabeth Clinton, Ella Stewart, Misty Walker, Holly Sparks, Jillian Ruize, Gina Behrends, and Nikki Ash—you ladies are my rock!

Thank you so much to Misty for being my right-hand woman always and forever! You always help me whenever I need it most. You're a great friend, an awesome lady, and one day I hope we can be tiny homes neighbors. One day we'll meet and I may suffocate you with my cuddles of appreciation. Love ya, boo!

A big thank you to my author friends who have given me your friendship and your support. You have no idea how much that means to me.

Thank you to all of my blogger friends both big and small that go above and beyond to always share my stuff. You all rock! #AllBlogsMatter

Jenn Wood with All About the Edits, thank you SO much for editing this book. You're amazing and I can't thank you enough! Love you!

Thank you Stacey Blake for being amazing as always when formatting my books and in general. I love you! I love you! I love you!

A big thanks to my PR gal, Nicole Blanchard. You are fabulous at what you do and keep me on track!

Lastly but certainly not least of all, thank you to all of the wonderful readers out there who are willing to hear my story and enjoy my characters like I do. It means the world to me!

ABOUT THE AUTHOR

K Webster is the *USA Today* bestselling author of over sixty romance books in many different genres including contemporary romance, historical romance, paranormal romance, dark romance, romantic suspense, taboo romance, and erotic romance. When not spending time with her hilarious and handsome husband and two adorable children, she's active on social media connecting with her readers.

Her other passions besides writing include reading and graphic design. K can always be found in front of her computer chasing her next idea and taking action. She looks forward to the day when she will see one of her titles on the big screen.

Join K Webster's newsletter to receive a couple of updates a month on new releases and exclusive content. To join, all you need to do is go here (www.authorkwebster.com).

Facebook:
www.facebook.com/authorkwebster

Blog:
authorkwebster.wordpress.com

Twitter:
twitter.com/KristiWebster

Email:
kristi@authorkwebster.com

Goodreads:
www.goodreads.com/user/show/10439773-k-webster

Instagram:
instagram.com/kristiwebster

K WEBSTER'S
Taboo World

two interconnected stories

BAD
BAD
BAD

two taboo treats

k webster

Bad Bad Bad

Two interconnected stories. Two taboo treats.

Brandt's Cherry Girl

He's old enough to be her father.
She's his best friend's daughter.
Their connection is off the charts.
And so very, very wrong.
This can't happen.
Oh, but it already is…

Sheriff's Bad Girl

He's the law and follows the rules.
She's wild and out of control.
His daughter's best friend is trouble.
And he wants to punish her…
With his teeth.

USA TODAY BESTSELLING AUTHOR

K WEBSTER

She's a hurdle in his way...
and he wants to jump her.

a taboo treat

COACH

LONG

Coach Long

Coach Everett Long has a chip on his shoulder.
Working every day with the man who stole his
fiancée leaves him pissed and on edge.
His temper is volatile and his attitude sucks.

River Banks is a funky-styled runner
with a bizarre past.
Starting over at a new school was supposed to
be easy…but she should have known better.
She likes to antagonize and tends to go after
what she's not supposed to have.

When the arrogant bully meets the strong-willed
brat, it sparks an illicit attraction.
Together, they heat up the track with
longing and desire.
Everything about their chemistry is wrong.
So why does it feel so right?

She's a hurdle in his way and, dear God does
he want to jump her.
Will she be worth the risk or
will he fall flat on his face?

Ex-Rated Attraction

I liked Caleb.

I like his dad more.

Miles Reynolds sent shocks through me the very first time I met him. With his full beard and sculpted ass, he's every inch a heroic, powerful Greek god.

He saved me from a bad situation and now he's all I can think of. Every minute of every hour of every day, I want that man.

He's warned me away, says I can't handle what he has to give.

But I know better.

Miles is exactly what I need—now, then and forever.

Mr. Blakely

It started as a job.

It turned into so much more.

Mr. Blakely is strict with his sons, but he's soft and gentle with me.

The powerful businessman is something else entirely when we're together.

Boss, teacher, lover…husband.

My hopes and dreams for the future have changed. I want—no, I need—him by my side.

a taboo treat

malfeasance

Judge Rowe
never had
a problem with
morality...
until her.

USA TODAY BESTSELLING AUTHOR
K WEBSTER

Malfeasance

Max Rowe always follows the rules.
A successful judge.
A single father.
A leader in the community.
Doing the right thing means everything.

But when he finds himself rescuing an incredibly
young woman,
everything he's worked hard for is quickly forgotten.
The only thing that matters is keeping her safe.
She's gorgeous, intelligent, and the ultimate
temptation.
Doing the wrong thing suddenly feels right.

Their chemistry is intense.
It's a romance no one will approve of, yet one they
can't ignore.
Hot, fast, and explosive.
Someone is going to get burned.

He'll give up everything for her...
because without her, he is nothing.

EASTON

K WEBSTER

Easton

A man who made countless mistakes.
A woman with a messy past.

He's tasked with helping her find her way.
She's lost in grief and self-doubt.

Together they begin something innocent…
Until it's not.

His freedom is at risk.
Her heart won't survive another break.

All rational thinking says they
should stay away from each other.
But neither are very good
at following the rules.

A deep, dark craving.
An overwhelming need.
A burn much hotter than any hell
they could ever be condemned to.

He'll give up everything for her…
because without her, he is nothing.

He likes her screams.
He likes them an awful lot.

Crybaby

a taboo treat

K WEBSTER

Crybaby

Stubborn.
Mouthy.
Brazen.
Two people with vicious tongues.
A desperate temptation neither can ignore.

An injury has changed her entire life.
She's crippled, hopeless, and angry.
And the only one who can lessen her pain is him.

Being the boss is sometimes a pain in the ass.
He's irritated, impatient, and doesn't play games.
Yet he's the only one willing to fight her…for her.

Daring.
Forbidden.
Out of control.
Someone is going to get hurt.
And, oh, how painfully sweet that will be.

lawn
BOYS
a taboo treat

The grass is greener where
he points his hose...

USA TODAY BESTSELLING AUTHOR
K WEBSTER

Lawn Boys

She's lived her life and it has been a good one.
Marriage. College. A family.
Slowly, though, life moved forward and left her at a
standstill.

Until the lawn boy barges into her world.
Bossy. Big. Sexy as hell.
A virile young male to remind her she's all woman.

Too bad she's twice his age.
Too bad he doesn't care.

She's older and wiser and more mature.
Which means absolutely nothing when he's invading
her space.

K WEBSTER

Principal Renner,
I've been *bad*.
Again.

a taboo treat

RENNER'S
Rules

Renner's Rules

I'm a bad girl.
I was sent away.
New house. New rules. New school.
Change was supposed to be…good.

Until I met him.

No one warned me Principal Renner would be so
hot.
I'd expected some old, graying man in a brown suit.
Not this.
Not well over six feet of lean muscle and piercing
green eyes.
Not a rugged-faced, ax-wielding lumberjack of a
man.

He's grouchy and rude and likes to boss me around.
I find myself getting in trouble just so he'll punish
me.
Especially with his favorite metal ruler.

Being bad never felt so good

K WEBSTER

Two people.
Their unraveling
marriage.
And they want
me to be...

the

GLUE

a taboo treat

The Glue

I'm a fixer. A lover. Always searching for the right fit.
And I come up empty every time.
My desires are unusual.
I don't feel whole until I'm in the middle, holding it
all together.
Which makes having a romantic relationship really
difficult.

Until them.
Two people. An unraveling marriage. Love on the
rocks.
And they want me.
To put them back together again.

Problem is, once they're fixed, where does that leave
me?
I sure as hell hope I stick like glue.

Made in the USA
Columbia, SC
18 October 2018